To Make a
KILLING

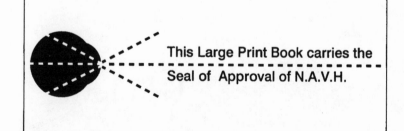

To Make a
KILLING

ROBERT J. CONLEY

Published in 2004 by arrangement with
Cherry Weiner Literary Agency.

Wheeler Large Print Western.

The text of this Large Print edition is unabridged.
Other aspects of the book may vary from the original edition.

Set in 16 pt. Plantin.

Printed in the United States on permanent paper.

ISBN 1-58724-624-4 (lg. print : sc : alk. paper)

Special thanks to
Bob L. Neal
and
Murv Jacob

As the Founder/CEO of NAVH, the only national health agency solely devoted to those who, although not totally blind, have an eye disease which could lead to serious visual impairment, I am pleased to recognize Thorndike Press★ as one of the leading publishers in the large print field.

Founded in 1954 in San Francisco to prepare large print textbooks for partially seeing children, NAVH became the pioneer and standard setting agency in the preparation of large type.

Today, those publishers who meet our standards carry the prestigious "Seal of Approval" indicating high quality large print. We are delighted that Thorndike Press is one of the publishers whose titles meet these standards. We are also pleased to recognize the significant contribution Thorndike Press is making in this important and growing field.

Lorraine H. Marchi, L.H.D.
Founder/CEO
NAVH

★ Thorndike Press encompasses the following imprints: Thorndike, Wheeler, Walker and Large Pr int Press.

Chapter

1

Go-Ahead Rider sopped the last of the gravy on his plate with a big fluffy biscuit. He stuffed it into his mouth, chewed, and swallowed it down. Then he leaned back away from the table, with both hands on his expanding belly, and took a deep breath.

"That was a mighty fine meal, Miz Tanner," he said.

"Thank you, Sheriff," said Lee Tanner. "I'm glad you enjoyed it, but I wish you'd call me Lee."

Rider smiled. "I'll try to remember that," he said.

George Tanner, who had been sitting across the table from Rider, stood up. He walked over to the stove and picked up the coffee pot, then went back to the table, behind and to the right of Exie Rider.

"More coffee, Exie?" he said.

"Yes," said Exie. "Thank you."

Rider was proud of Exie's progress with English. She had not spoken a word of the strange language when they got married and had not seemed interested in learning. But when the children had started to school, they had come home with English words, and Exie had begun to pick some up from them. Then Rider had hired the mixed-blood, George Tanner, as his deputy, and George had married Lee Hunt, a schoolteacher and another mixed-blood. Neither George nor Lee could speak Cherokee, so when the Tanners and Riders started visiting each other socially, Exie had started concentrating a little harder on her English, and she was getting to be pretty good at it. Rider was proud of her.

George had refilled all the cups and replaced the pot, but he did not resume his seat.

"You want to sit outside?" he said to Rider. "I've got some chairs out back."

"Sounds good to me," said Rider. "I'd like a smoke."

The two men went out the back door carrying their cups, and Lee began to clear the table. Exie stood up and collected the dishes there in front of her.

"That's all right," said Lee. "Sit back down and enjoy your coffee."

"I'll help you," said Exie.

"I'm glad you could come tonight. George admires the sheriff so much."

"George is a good man." said Exie, "Me and Rider, we're both happy for you. And the children like you, too. Both of you."

"I wonder what your children are doing?"

"Oh, they find something."

The Rider children, eleven-year-old Tootie and her seven-year-old brother Buster, were on their hands and knees about fifty yards behind the Tanner house carefully watching a turtle who had shut himself up tight inside his shell when they approached too close for his comfort. They had, as usual, finished eating long before the grown-ups, and had asked to be excused to go outside and play.

When Rider and George went outside to the chairs, they saw the children.

"Now what do you suppose they're up to?" asked George.

"Ain't no telling," said Rider, taking a seat. He sipped his coffee and leaned over to place the cup on the ground beside his chair. "George," he said, "you got yourself a fine woman in there. She's good looking, and real smart, and she can cook, too. That's almost more than a man deserves."

"I'd have married Lee without your approval," said George, "but I'm glad you like her. Thank you."

Rider reached into a side pocket of his black vest and pulled out a pipe and a tobacco pouch. He filled the pipe bowl and put the pouch away. Then, pipe stem between his teeth, he pulled a small tin out of his pocket, opened it, and extracted a wooden match. He closed the tin and put it away. Then he struck the

9

match on the side of the chair and lit his pipe.

"You never did tell me what the judge said this afternoon," said George.

"He said we ain't got the budget. That's all."

"No extra help."

"Nope. We got to do with what we got."

"Well," said George, "it won't be easy. The council meeting starts in just two days."

"I expect," said Rider, "that folks'll start pouring into town tomorrow, filling up the hotels, camping down along the creek."

"Do you really expect even more people than usual to come into Tahlequah for this session?"

"I expect so," said Rider. "It's a hot issue. A lot of folks are mad about it."

"The U.S. wants six million more acres of our land," said George, "for a reservation for the Pawnees."

"Yeah, and it's worse than that. They figure that since it's only for Indians, they'll just only pay us half the fair market value of the land."

"And the Cherokee Nation was never even consulted," said George. "They never even asked us what we thought about it."

"Why should they change their habits now?" said Rider. "Boley said, too, that the commissioners who are going to come down here to assess the land have already gathered up in Lawrence, Kansas."

Rider reached down for his coffee cup,

brought it up to his lips, and took a long sip.

"Well, what can our council do about it?" asked George.

"Most likely nothing," said Rider. "I expect they'll draft a letter of protest to send to Washington. That's about all."

"So we've got a hot issue being debated by the council and a town full of people pouring in and no extra help to keep the peace," said George.

"That's about the way it looks," said Rider, "but there ain't no sense in fretting over it. We just got to do our job the best way we can."

"Yeah."

The children suddenly jumped up and came running toward the two men. When they got close, Buster held out the turtle, still clamped firmly shut, toward Rider.

"Look what we found," he said.

"What is it?" said Rider, squinting as if he couldn't tell.

"*Ulinawi*," said Buster.

"It's a turtle," said Tootie, "but it won't come out of its shell."

"Well," said Rider, "I reckon he's scared of you."

"We won't hurt him," said Buster.

"I guess he don't know that. Put him down over yonder and stand back for a little bit. I bet he'll come out then."

"He'll run away," said Buster.

"He can't run very fast."

11

"Come on, Buster," said Tootie. "Put him down."

Buster ran a few feet away and put the turtle on the ground. Then he and his sister ran back to stand near Rider.

"When's he going to come out?" said Tootie.

"Just wait," said Rider. "Be patient."

Then the creature opened up. It poked its head out and looked around. Its legs came out, and it started to walk.

"Look," cried Tootie. "There he goes."

Buster ran after the turtle.

"Let him go," said Tootie, running after her brother.

"No," said Buster. "I'm going to take him home with me."

George laughed.

"It would be nice to have no more worries than they do," he said.

Rider puffed his pipe without comment for a moment. The pipe went out and he tapped it on the side of the chair to knock loose the dottle. The back door of the house came open, and Exie stepped out. She was followed by Lee.

"Rider," said Exie, "we better go home. It's getting late."

Rider stood up, poking his pipe back into the vest pocket. He bent over to pick up the empty coffee cup.

"Here," said George, standing up, "I'll take that."

Rider handed George the cup, then looked out toward where the children were running.

"Buster. Tootie," he called.

"What?" yelled Buster.

"Come on. It's time to go home."

"I'm taking my turtle," said Buster.

"Okay."

"We're real glad you came," said Lee.

"It was real nice, Miz, uh, Lee," said Rider. "Thanks a lot. George is a lucky man. I told him so, too."

"Thank you," said Lee.

"We'll have to do this again," said George.

"Next time," said Exie, "you come to our house. Okay?"

As the Riders started walking toward the road that would lead them on to their house, George stepped over beside his wife and put an arm around her shoulders.

"They're fine people," said Lee.

"Yeah," said George. "They turned him down, Lee. The judge told him we don't have enough money in the budget."

"You mean for the extra deputies he requested?"

"Yeah. How can they turn down a man like Captain Go-Ahead Rider?"

George used Rider's wartime rank, as many people still did, for the sheriff's reputation had been made originally during the Civil War, when he had been a captain in the Cherokee Home Guard.

"Well," said Lee, "if they don't have the money, they don't have the money, I guess. Do you really think you'll need the extra help?"

"It's always hectic in town when the council's in session," said George, "but Rider thinks that with this land issue on the agenda, it'll be even worse. Lots of people will come into town because of that. But that's not what worries me."

Lee didn't say anything. She waited for George to continue.

"Rider doesn't ask for help very often. When he does ask, he really needs it."

Chapter

2

Matthew Thomson was puffed up. He was about to make a killing, and, by God, he thought, it was about time. He was due, long overdue, in fact. Being a citizen and resident of the Cherokee Nation, where land was held in common, there was no way to profit from land speculation. At least that had been his belief until when, too late, he had seen E. C. Boudinot and some others manage to do exactly that when the railroads had gone through. But Thomson had missed that boat, so he decided that he would have to come up with something else, some other way to make his fortune.

He knew that the council was going to meet and consider its reaction to the latest attempt of the federal government to take away more Cherokee land, but he couldn't see any way to profit from that business.

And, of course, it had not escaped his attention that several of the prominent Cherokee politicians had managed to accumulate considerable personal wealth. He did not know exactly how they had done so, but it seemed to him that one should be able to become a politician and then find out how to take full advantage of his position. So he had run for a seat on the national council from his own Delaware District, but unhappily, he had lost the election.

Thomson had a home in the Delaware District of the Cherokee Nation, just below the southern boundary of the lands marked off by the federal government for the use of the Senecas, Quapaws, Peorias, Modocs, Ottawas, Shawnees, Wyandots, Tonkawas, Poncas, and Oto-Missourias. The land he had use of was also nestled up against the border between the Cherokee Nation and the state of Missouri. He farmed a little, and he ran a few head of cattle, but the land there was not really suited to either farming or to raising cattle. But then, neither was Thomson's disposition. He considered himself rather to be cut out more for the role of gentleman farmer.

But now at last he had figured out the way to make his fortune. It had come to him following an incident that took place when he allowed a few head of his scrawny cattle to wander off of his property. Someone had reported the loose cattle to Captain Fish, the sheriff of Delaware District, and Fish had, according to law, rounded up the cattle and posted a notice. When the proper amount of time had passed, and Thomson had failed to respond, Fish had sold the cattle at public auction.

Then, when it was too late, Thomson had complained to Fish, and Fish had taken a ride out to Thomson's place. There he had discovered that Thomson's fences did not conform to the requirements of law, and he had ordered Thomson to correct that problem. Thomson had not only lost his cattle, but he had been required to spend money fixing his fences. He had been angry and frustrated by all that, and it had made him want to get drunk.

In the Cherokee Nation, the use of "ardent spirits" was strictly forbidden, but being close to the Missouri state line, Thomson had gone to the nearest town in that state and had himself a good roaring drunk, a real toot.

It had been the next day, after he sobered up, that his business plan had come to him. It was a good plan, and he was proud of himself for having schemed it up. Liquor was illegal in the Cherokee Nation, but, of course, there were people who dealt in it anyway on the sly. There were always men who wanted a drink, and when one man is willing to pay for something, there is always another who is more than willing to supply that commodity.

Thomson well knew that there were those

who smuggled liquor into the Cherokee Nation from Arkansas or Missouri or Kansas. He also knew that there were those inside the Cherokee Nation who made their own product, either to use for themselves or to sell to others. There was certainly no shortage of liquor in the Cherokee Nation.

But there was also, as far as he knew, no one smart enough to have embarked on a grand scheme for dealing in large quantities of good-quality, high-dollar booze. And it occurred to him that he was the man to do it. It would be a little risky, of course, but he planned carefully, and the location of his property was the key to the whole enterprise.

Thomson's neighbor just across the state line on the Missouri side was a white man named Joseph Carter. Thomson's property and Carter's were separated from each other only by the imaginary line that divided the Cherokee Nation from the state of Missouri. And the two men had been good neighbors, almost good friends. They had hunted together once in a while. They had bought and sold back and forth between them dogs, hogs, and even a few cattle. They had even gotten drunk together on a couple of memorable occasions.

So one day, after having gone over his carefully formulated plan several times searching for flaws, correcting, refining, Thomson had paid a visit to Carter and proposed a partnership. Thomson would acquire large quantities of whiskey from some reputable, legitimate distributor, and they would store the stuff at Carter's place in Carter's big barn. So far everything was perfectly legal.

Then Thomson would line up several local dealers on the Cherokee Nation side of the line. They would come to him for the goods. He and Carter would bring whatever amount the dealer could pay for across the line, never going out on any public roads. They would conclude the transaction on Thomson's property, and the local dealer would go on his way. Even if one of them should get caught and spill the beans, if the law came to Thomson's place to investigate they would find nothing incriminating on his property, and they would not be able to go across the line into Missouri, outside of their jurisdiction, to investigate. The law on the Missouri side was no worry. No laws would be broken over there.

"It's foolproof," he had said to Carter.

Carter had simply stared at his table in deep and seemingly painful thought.

"Well," Thomson had said, "are you with me? We'll both get rich."

"I don't know," Carter had mumbled. "I never thought I'd go into business with no Indian. I don't mean no offense. Nothing against you personal. I just never really quite seen myself that way. You know?"

"Oh, hell, give me a piece of paper and a pencil," Thomson had said, and Carter had rummaged around and found them. Thomson had drawn a circle on the paper and then had begun dividing it up as if it were a pie.

"There's fourths," he said, "and then there's eighths. One more time. There's sixteenths. Now I'm going to slice one of these here sixteenths in half. There you have a thirty-second. You see that?"

"Yeah. Sure. I ain't totally ignorant, you know."

"That thirty-second there," Thomson had said, "that's how much Indian I am. One damn thirty-second. Hell, do I look like an Indian to you?"

"Well, not really. I can't think of no other Indians I ever seen with a bald spot on top of their heads." He chuckled. "I guess you're right. It don't really matter. Only just one other thing then."

"What's that, Buddy?"

"Where you going to get the money to buy the first load of whiskey?"

Thomson had looked a bit troubled by that question, but he had only remarked, "Let me worry about that. Okay?"

And sure enough, here he was, sitting across the table from Albert Palmer, one of the biggest distributors of quality whiskey in the business, in the lounge of the Southern Hotel on Walnut Street in St. Louis, Missouri. He had come to St. Louis by way of Seneca, the end of the line for the Atlantic and Pacific Railroad, just north of Carter's place and just across the border from the lands of the Senecas and all those other small tribes. It had been his first trip on a train, and he had enjoyed it immensely. It would not be his last, he told himself. From now on he would be traveling in style wherever he might go.

He had come up with the money, miraculously, he told himself, when his uncle died, leaving Thomson his entire estate. It was not as much money as Thomson would have liked for this first deal with Palmer, but it would do. It would have to. It had gotten him a new suit and a round-trip ticket on the A and P, and he was staying in the fabulous Southern Hotel. The A and P itself had its headquarters in that very building, and Palmer was also staying there. All of that was important to Thomson. He had to impress on Palmer that he was a man of means, a good businessman, and a safe risk.

"You understand, Mr. Palmer," Thomson was saying, "that this first purchase is just a kind of experiment. I need to find out which brands will be the most popular with my clients, and I need to find out how the new routes will work. The next order will be much larger. My partner and I have a warehouse for storage, and it's my intention to fill it up to capacity."

"With my products," said Palmer.

"Of course," said Thomson. "The very best available."

"More champagne, Mr. Thomson?" said Palmer, smiling and lifting the bottle.

"Yes. Thank you. When can I expect delivery of this first shipment?"

"I can have it on the next train to Seneca, Mr. Thomson. From there it's your problem."

"It's no problem," said Thomson. "I'll have wagons there to meet it, pick it up, and take it to my warehouse."

Palmer had poured the drinks, and Thomson lifted his glass.

"Here's to a long and profitable relationship, Mr. Palmer," he said.

Palmer lifted his own glass and touched it to Thomson's with a clink.

"To money," he said.

Thomson had just drained the last drop from his glass when he was startled by the sound of a voice calling his name.

"Matt. Matt Thomson, by God," it said.

No one in St. Louis knew him. He was far from home. Who the hell could it be? he thought as he turned his head to look.

"By God, Matt, I never expected to run into nobody from back home in the old Cherokee Nation way out here in Saint

Looey. Put her there, partner."

Thomson recognized Eli Martin. Martin, like Thomson, was a mixed-blood citizen of the Cherokee Nation. Thomson knew Martin, but not well. He knew that Martin had the background of a cowboy but had become in recent years some kind of a broker between the ranchers in the Cherokee Nation and the cattle buyers in the east. He must be here on business, thought Thomson. He stood up and shook Martin's hand, but not enthusiastically.

"Look, Martin," he said, his voice low, "I'm here on an important business deal."

"Hell, me too. Shit, I couldn't afford no trip to Saint Looey just for the hell of it. Let me buy you and your friend there a drink."

"No," said Thomson. "No thanks. Some other time maybe. We're really busy here."

"I always mix drinks and business. It's the only way to go. Let me buy y'all one round. Come on. What do you say?"

"Martin," said Thomson, losing what was left of his patience, "you're butting in where you're not wanted. Leave me alone here, will you?"

"Well, hell, yes, by God, if that's the way you want it. Just sit your raw red ass back down and relax. I ain't going to hang around where I ain't wanted. Hell of a thing, though. The only two Cherokees in this whole goddamned big city, and you won't even have a drink with me. And me offering to buy them.

I ain't forgetting this, Matthew Thomson, sir. To hell with you."

Martin turned and left the lounge. He wasn't exactly staggering, but he did seem to be a little unsteady on his feet. Thomson stared after him as he resumed his seat. He fought off an urge to follow the man. He couldn't follow him, though, and leave Palmer there alone with no explanation. It wouldn't look right.

"What was all that?" said Palmer. "Any problem?"

"What?" said Thomson. "Oh. No. No problem. It was nothing. Just a man from home. He wanted to join us and buy us some drinks. I sent him away."

"I wouldn't have minded," said Palmer. "It was someone from home and —"

"He's a disreputable sort of fellow," said Thomson. "I don't really associate with him even back home. No reason I should be bothered with him just because we're away from home."

"Oh, I see. Well, I think our business is just about concluded, don't you? That leaves us with only this bottle to finish before we call it a night. Right?"

"Right."

When the two businessmen parted company for the evening, Thomson started to look for Martin. He would have to do something, he told himself. He couldn't afford to have Martin telling anyone about having seen him with Palmer. This business with Palmer had to be kept a strict secret. Conviction for the selling of booze in the Cherokee Nation carried stiff sentences, jail terms and heavy fines, confiscation of property, and the destruction of all of the illegal inventory. Exposure by that fool Martin could mean ruin before the business even got started.

He checked at the desk and found out that Martin was not registered there. He walked up and down the streets without catching sight of him. He checked other nearby bars and hotels, but there was no sign of Eli Martin.

"Damn," he said. It had never occurred to him that anyone he knew would see him in St. Louis. What a hell of a damned coincidence for that Martin to walk in on him like that. He had to find him.

He didn't know just exactly what he would do if he did find him, yet he felt compelled to continue to search for him. He felt as if he had to do something. There was just too much at stake.

He searched well into the night before he gave it up. He had an early train to catch in the morning. He would just have to hope for the best, or he would have to deal somehow with Eli Martin back in the Cherokee Nation.

Chapter
3

The train ride back to Seneca seemed especially long to Matt Thomson. He was worried about having been seen in St. Louis by Eli Martin. He tried to take his mind off the problem by reading the copy of the *St. Louis Democrat* he had picked up back at the depot in the city, but that didn't work for long. He couldn't keep his mind on the stories. He would finish one and then catch himself wondering what it was he had just read.

Damn that Martin, he said to himself. He tried to remember where Martin lived, and he wasn't even sure he had ever known. Where had he run into the man before? He knew him, but from where? It was no use. Martin was just one of those people that Thomson knew enough to say hello to if he happened to run into him somewhere.

Martin worked with cattlemen, big ranchers. Logic told Thomson, then, that Martin must live somewhere in Cooweescoowee District. Possibly the extreme western or northern reaches of Delaware District, but more than likely over the line into Cooweescoowee. None of the rest of the Cherokee Nation was really suited to the cattle business, and for sure, all of the big cattlemen were in Cooweescoowee.

But then why, Thomson asked himself again, did he even know Martin? He had hardly ever been to Cooweescoowee District in his whole life? He had no reason to go there. He didn't even like that damn flat prairie country. And even when he had campaigned for a council position, he had not gotten much into the parts of his own district that bordered Cooweescoowee. Tahlequah, he thought. It must be from Tahlequah that he knew Martin.

Everyone goes to Tahlequah at one time or another. Having come up with that thought, he was almost sure that he could remember specific occasions when he had seen, even talked with Martin in Tahlequah, and that reminded him again that a national council meeting was scheduled for Tahlequah, the Cherokee Nation capital, in just a few days.

Like many citizens of the Cherokee Nation, Thomson usually went to Tahlequah when the council was in session. He told himself that he was a concerned citizen, and that he was interested in the actions of the council. After all, they were the lawmaking body of his nation, and he had to live under the laws they passed.

He might even find an opportunity to voice his opinion of some matter or other, and it was also in the back of his mind that he might decide to try for a council position again one of these days. It certainly couldn't hurt anything for him to be known around the capital as an astute, public minded, politically savvy individual.

He decided that he would give the paperwork on the whiskey shipment to his partner, Joseph Carter, and have Carter show up to meet the train, claim the goods, and get them hauled to the warehouse. He would give Carter enough money to hire the necessary wagons and drivers to get the job done, and if Carter balked at the idea, he would say that it was necessary for him to be in Tahlequah during the council session for a couple of reasons.

The council might pass some laws that would affect their new business, and if that should happen, he would know about it right away by hanging around during the meeting. Also, he would say, almost everybody goes to Tahlequah for these meetings, and therefore it would be the best time for him to contact his local salesmen or dealers. It would work. Carter was gullible. Besides, it was all true.

And there was another reason, one that he would keep to himself. No one else needed to know, not even Carter. He might see Martin in Tahlequah during the council meeting, and he still felt that it was urgent for him to locate Martin. He still wasn't at all sure what he would do or say to Martin when he found the man, but he knew that he had to do something.

Riding the train back toward Seneca, Missouri, he pondered that question. What would he do? Would he just walk up to Martin and say, "Eli, old friend, I'd like for you to forget that you ever saw me in St. Louis"? That didn't seem likely to do much good. He might try to engage Martin in conversation and try to learn whether or not the cowboy knew the identity of Albert Palmer. After all, he told himself, there might not be any real problem. So what if I was seen in St. Louis? That's no crime. And if Martin was unaware of the identity of his contact there, what difference if Martin had seen him?

But would Martin confide in him? He had been, he realized, rather rude to Martin in a public place, and Martin had gone away mad, had even threatened him, in a way. Far from sitting down with him for a cordial conversation, Martin might just punch him in the nose, or worse.

When the A and P at last arrived at Seneca, Thomson was no closer than ever to the answer to his problem. He still felt, though, that he had to locate Eli Martin one way or another and resolve this dilemma somehow.

He disembarked from the train at the Seneca station with his newspaper under his right arm and his small traveling valise in his left hand. He walked straight to the livery stable where he had left his horse and saddle, paid the man for the boarding, saddled the horse, mounted up, and headed south.

He rode straight to Joseph Carter's farm and tied up in front of the house. Carter stepped out on the porch to meet him.

"Howdy, Matt," said Carter. "How was the trip?"

"Good," said Thomson. "Our first shipment will be on the train tomorrow. But I've got a couple of samples in here."

He grinned as he held up his valise, and as soon as Carter caught on, he too grinned.

"Well, come on in," he said, "and let's sample your samples."

Thomson followed Carter into the house and over to the table where they each took a chair. Thomson put his valise on the table and opened it up. He reached in and pulled out two bottles of whiskey and set them on the table side by side.

"Hot damn," said Carter. "Let's have it."

"Well, how about some glasses?" said Thomson. "This here ain't rotgut, you know."

"Oh, yeah. Hell, I wasn't thinking. I'll just get them."

Thomson opened one bottle while Carter

was getting the glasses. Then he poured each of the two glasses half full. The two partners then lifted their glasses in a toast.

"Here's mud in your eye, by God," said Carter.

Thomson decided to let it go at that, tipped up his glass and tasted the whiskey. Carter took a gulp of his.

"That's fine whiskey," said Thomson. "We ought to be able to get top dollar for that stuff in the Cherokee Nation. Hell, when we get this business going real good, we might even expand down into the Creek Nation and the other nations. We might just spread our business on through the whole Indian Territory."

Carter smacked his lips and grinned another of his broad grins.

"Hell, yes," he said. "We might just as well go on and think big. You'll never get big by thinking little, will you?"

Thomson poured Carter another drink. His own was hardly touched.

"This is going to be big, Joe," he said. "You mark my words. We're going to be rich, you and me. Yes sir. We're going to be rich men."

He poured Carter three drinks before he had finished his own first one, and then he quit. He put the cork back in the bottle and the bottle back in the valise.

"Listen, Joe," he said. "I've got to be in

31

Tahlequah day after tomorrow. I'll have to leave first thing in the morning in order to get there on time. Now our whiskey is going to be here tomorrow on the train at Seneca. Here's the time it gets in right here on this bill of lading here. You see it?"

He pulled a piece of paper out of his pocket and laid it on the table in front of Carter.

"Yeah," said Carter. "I see it. Right there."

"That bill there also gives you the right to pick up that shipment. Now, you'll need some wagons and some drivers. I figure it'll take four of each. That is, unless you think you can handle one wagon yourself."

"I can drive a goddamned wagon as good as anyone else I know," said Carter, "and I got a good one right out there in the barn."

"Then hire three more," said Thomson, digging into a pocket for some bills. He put the money on the table. "This here will cover it," he said. "Now, can I trust you with that? Can I leave it to you to get it done right?"

"Hell yes. I'll do her. Don't worry about a damn thing."

Thomson rode on home and put his horse away. Inside his house, alone, he tossed the newspaper onto a small table in the corner of the room. He put the valise on his bed and sat down beside it, opening it up. He took out the two bottles of whiskey and set them side by side on his bedside table. For a long moment, he sat staring at the two bottles, and he thought about Eli Martin.

"The son of a bitch," he said. "The drunken —"

And then it came to him, the answer he had struggled for so long to find. He picked up the partly used bottle and carried it outside, where he poured its remaining contents out onto the ground. Then he went back in the house and put the bottle back beside the other one. He dumped the dirty clothes out of his valise into a corner of the room, found a fresh change of clothes in his bureau drawer, and put those into the valise along with the unopened bottle of whiskey.

He went to his wood stove, stuffed in some sticks, and lit a fire. He took a pot and went outside to the rain barrel to fill it with water, then took it back in and put it on the stove, In a cabinet he found some sassafras root, which he tossed into the water.

While waiting for the water to boil, he found a pencil and paper and sat down at his dining table where he sketched for a few minutes, scratching his head and wrinkling his brow.

He got up and went back to the bureau and opened another drawer. He tossed a few things out of the drawer until he came up with what he was looking for, an old pair of thick buffalo-hide mittens, heavy mittens with the fur on the outside. He took one of the mittens and put it in his valise.

Sitting back down at the table, he picked up the pencil again and started to write a list.

cane pole
twine
hooks (4?)
gun?!?
bullet, just one

He stood up in order to reach into his pocket and pull out his cash. He had spent most of it on the whiskey order and the hotel and the rail trip. Then he had given some to Carter for the wagons and drivers. He hadn't left himself much. Of course, he expected to make plenty of money soon enough, but he needed some immediately. He counted the cash and decided that it would do. It would have to.

He heard the water boiling on the stove, and he got up to take a look at it. It would have to go a while longer. It needed some color. Well, that was all right. He still had a couple of other things to do.

He rummaged again in another drawer until he found a long, thin strip of rawhide. He tossed it into the valise. Then he lit a lantern and carried it outside. He walked around behind his house to a small shed. Inside the shed he found a long river-cane fishing pole. He carried that with him back into the house and tossed it down on the table.

"Ha," he said. He put down the lantern, sat down at the table, and picked up the pencil again. He drew a line through the words *cane pole*, another through *twine*, and another through *hooks*. The only items remaining on the list were *gun* and *bullet*. He wadded up the piece of paper, got up and stepped over to the stove. Opening the stove door, he tossed the paper into the fire, then shut the door. He looked at the boiling water on top of the stove and saw that it was beginning to develop a little color. It was starting to look like tea. He would let it go yet for a while longer.

Back at the table, he unstrung the fishing pole, took off the hook and dropped it on the table, and rolled the twine that had been the fishing line up into a small ball. He checked the eyelets that the line had been strung through and found them all still firmly set. He took the ball of twine over to the valise and tossed it in. Then he checked the brew on the stove again. It looked all right. He took the pot off the stove and set it aside to allow the tea to cool.

Everything was all right. Everything except the gun and the bullet. He would want a lightweight weapon. A single shot would be all right, he thought, and it should be inexpensive. His funds were limited, and besides that, it should probably be thrown away. He wondered if he would be required to buy a whole box of bullets for the gun when all he really wanted was one. Well, he would worry about that when the time came.

He would not want to buy the gun in Tahlequah nor anywhere on the way between his house and Tahlequah. He decided that he would have to make a side trip just to buy the gun. Where should he go for that purpose? Back to Seneca? Why not? It wasn't too far. He could ride up to Seneca and then down to Tahlequah easily enough all in one day. That might put him into Tahlequah after dark, and it might be difficult for him to get a room by then, but he would just have to take a chance on that.

He checked his tea and found that it had cooled enough. He went over to the bedside table to get the empty whiskey bottle, which he then carried to the kitchen counter where he had left the pan of tea. He got a funnel out of a drawer and used it to pour the tea into the bottle. Then he stood back and studied the bottle of tea. The color was not bad. It looked enough like a bottle of booze to pass. He found the cork and put it back in the bottle. Then he put that bottle into the valise with the other one. There was nothing more he could do until morning, so he got himself ready for bed. Tomorrow would be a long day.

Chapter 4

Matthew Thomson was up before the sun, and it was still gray dawn when he rode away from his house on Old Jeb, his favorite saddle horse, named respectfully for Jeb Stuart. During the Civil War, Thomson had ridden with Stand Watie's Confederate Cherokees, and Old Jeb's name was just one example of his continued loyalty to that lost cause.

Thomson rode Old Jeb across his own property and then across that of his partner Carter. The trip back to Seneca was considerably shortened that way. In Seneca he located a gun shop, and after hastily looking over what was available in there, he selected a second-hand Jacob Rupertus single-shot .41 caliber 1870-model pocket pistol. It had a stud trigger, but Thomson tested it and found that it had a light and easy pull. It should work. He was pleasantly surprised to find out that he was able to purchase one single .41 caliber bullet. He put the pistol and the bullet into his valise and resumed his journey.

It was a long day's ride from Seneca to

Tahlequah, so Thomson alternately pushed Old Jeb and then eased off so as not to wear the animal out. Old Jeb was a good horse, and Thomson knew what kind of pace he could handle well. During the intervals of easy riding, Thomson ran over and over again in his mind the details of his plan.

There were only two uncertainties in the plan that he could think of. First, he couldn't be sure that Martin would be in Tahlequah. It seemed likely that he would be, but there was no guarantee. That was Thomson's biggest worry. The next uncertainty was how Martin would react to Thomson's approach, but Thomson thought he would be able to handle that if only he was fortunate enough to see the man. He rehearsed in his mind what he would say.

He would act pleased to see Martin, and he would apologize for his behavior in St. Louis. Then he would offer to make amends by sharing a couple of bottles of good whiskey with Martin. The apology would appeal to Martin's pride, the rest of the approach to his love of good whiskey. Actually, Thomson had no idea what Martin's preference in liquor might be, but he had seen the man drunk in a high-toned lounge in St. Louis and so assumed that quality booze would appeal to him.

If he could get that far with Martin, he told himself, the rest should be easy. Tahlequah would be crowded with people, and that meant that Thomson would have to be careful not to be seen involved in anything that might be incriminating. But it also meant that his chances for not being seen and not being suspected of anything were better. A man in a crowd is seldom noticed, he thought. He tried playing the devil's advocate, looking for flaws in his own plan, but he could find none that he could not also come up with solutions to. It was still a good plan, and he was proud of it.

He arrived in Tahlequah after dark. He had figured that it would take about that much time. He stopped by the National Hotel and the Capitol Hotel, and he found that neither one had a vacancy. He was a little disappointed, but he had expected as much, so he shrugged it off. He rode through the main part of town on Muskogee Avenue to the livery stable at the other end. It, too, was full.

He turned east and rode to the edge of Wolfe Creek, and, just as he had expected, there were people camped all along the creek. He headed back north, riding slowly, watching for a space he could nudge himself into. He had not gone far beyond the two-story brick capitol building that was the center of Tahlequah before he found it, a space between two tents. The tent fronts faced the creek. He rode Old Jeb into the space, and then he was able to see two small fires, one burning in front of each of the tents. Two women sat in front of one tent, a man and a woman in front of the other.

"*'Siyo,*" said Thomson, using up about a third of his Cherokee vocabulary.

"*'Siyo,*" said the others.

"Do any of you speak English?"

"I do," said the man.

"Is this space taken?"

"No, I don't think so. I ain't seen no one there."

Thomson looked toward the other tent, but the women sitting there didn't seem to understand what was going on. He turned back to the man who had spoken to him in English.

"Do you talk Cherokee?" he asked.

"Yeah. Better than this white man's language."

"Would you mind asking your neighbors over here if it's all right with them if I camp out here?"

The man said something in Cherokee to the women in front of the other tent, and they gave him a brief answer. Then the man spoke again to Thomson in English.

"They said it's okay if you want to," he said. "Just go on and take it. It's okay."

"Thanks," said Thomson, and he climbed down out of the saddle.

"You going to do some fishing?" asked the man at the tent.

"What?" said Thomson, and then he remembered his long cane pole. It was tied to the saddle and was, of course, conspicuous. "Oh. Oh, yeah. I thought I might try to get in a little fishing."

"It wouldn't be any good here," said the man. "Too many kids running in and out of the creek."

"Yeah. I'll have to go upstream some, I guess."

Thomson put down his valise, took the cane pole loose and put it down, untied a blanket roll from behind the saddle and tossed it on the ground, then unsaddled Old Jeb. He didn't bother tying the horse or hobbling him. He just let the reins trail on the ground. Old Jeb wouldn't go far like that. Thomson noted with pleasure that the grass was lush there by the creek. Old Jeb would do just fine.

He spread his blanket roll on the ground with the saddle at the head for a pillow. That and Old Jeb together should make it obvious to anyone who might come by that this spot was taken.

He considered for a moment the fact that someone had taken notice of his cane pole, but he decided that it made no difference. No one would ever manage to put together his scheme. There was lots of fishing in those parts, and there were lots of cane poles. He forgot about it.

He had decided that he would leave his camp and walk on over to Muskogee Avenue to see if he could find some place still open where he could get something to eat. He still had a little cash left. He hadn't had any food all day, and he was hungry. But just then the man at the tent spoke to him again.

"Hey, neighbor. We still got some good food left over here. You hungry?"

Thomson hesitated but only for a second.

"Well, yeah," he said. "Matter of fact, I'm just about to starve to death. I was just fixing to walk on downtown to see if I could find some place to eat."

"All them places charge too much money," said the other man. "Besides, I think they're all closed down now. You might as well have some of this here. It's fresh and hot, and my wife here is a real good cook."

"Well, thank you very much. That's real kind of you."

Thomson strolled on over in front of the tent. The man had pulled a couple of logs up by his fire to use as seats, and Thomson sat down on one.

"I hate to intrude," he said.

"Ain't no trouble," said the man. "The food's all cooked, and we've all ate. Our two boys ran off down the creek with some other kids. We're just sitting around here."

The woman handed Thomson a bowl of bean soup.

"*Wado*," he said. He knew but a few basic words of the Cherokee language: hello, thank you, a few others.

"*Howa,*" she said. She ducked back inside the tent and came out a moment later with a plate. She dug into another pot there by the fire and got some bacon, which she put on the plate. Then from under a cloth she took out some fried bread. She handed that plate to Thomson. His mouth was full, so he just nodded to her as he took it and placed it on the log there beside himself. By then the man had poured a cup of coffee, and he put that on the log beside the plate.

"There you go," the man said.

"Thanks," said Thomson. "Say, this is real good. Would you tell your wife I said so, and tell her I sure do appreciate it?"

The man spoke to the woman in Cherokee. She smiled and gave a brief response. Thomson smiled back at her, nodding his head as he ate. He had a second bowl of bean soup and plenty of bacon and bread and coffee. As he was finishing up another cup of coffee, the man pulled a watch out of his pocket, turned it toward the fire so he could see the face, tucked it back in his pocket, and stood up.

"Well," he said, "I'm going to have to get going. I got to relieve a man. We work in shifts. See you around, neighbor."

He spoke to his wife in Cherokee, strapped on a gun belt, from which dangled a six-gun in a holster, around his waist, picked up a Winchester rifle, and turned to walk toward

43

town. Thomson drained his coffee cup, put the cup down, and stood up. He eyed his host suspiciously, for he knew that it was against the law to carry firearms.

"I better be going too," he said. "Thanks again for the hospitality."

He gave the woman a nod and started to walk alongside the man. As they crossed through the area of Thomson's campsite, Thomson picked up his valise. He spoke to Old Jeb and gave him a pat.

"Good-looking horse," said the man.

"Old Jeb," said Thomson. "He's the best."

"He looks good all right. Well, I see you later."

"I think I'll just check the town over before I turn in," said Thomson. "See what I can see. Which way you headed?"

"Downtown," said the man. "Capitol building."

He didn't offer any other explanation. Just like a damn full-blood, thought Thomson. Generous to a fault with everything but information. He had eaten the man's food but did not even know his name. And now the man was going heavily armed to relieve someone at the capitol building. What the hell did that mean?

Ha, he thought. Of course. He's a special deputy on duty at the capitol for the duration of the council meeting.

Thomson had a moment of panic. His valise

contained a bottle of whiskey, what looked like two bottles of whiskey, and here he had camped right beside a deputy. Now he was walking along with the man as if they were friends and carrying that valise. Possession of that whiskey could cost him dearly if it happened to be discovered, and, of course, such an unfortunate occurrence would put an abrupt end to all his other plans.

Then he recalled the cane pole. He had dismissed that earlier as a minor incident, something of no importance, but now that he realized it had been a lawman who had noticed the pole, he worried again. Of course, what he had told himself before was still true. There was nothing illegal or incriminating about a fishing pole, nothing unusual even.

And then he thought, what better neighbor for me to have? What better friend? If I'm friendly with the law and they with me, the less likely anyone will be to suspect me of anything. The thought forced a smile to his face, and he was glad for the cover of darkness.

They walked along side by side in silence until they reached the square on which the capitol stood. Thomson could see a deputy standing on the square just inside the low rail fence. His temporary companion headed toward that man.

"See you, neighbor," the man said.

"Yeah," said Thomson. "And thanks again, friend."

He stopped walking and stood watching as the man approached the other deputy. The two lawmen exchanged a few words in the Cherokee language, then the one being relieved started walking away. He walked in the direction of Thomson. As he passed Thomson by, he touched the brim of his hat.

"*'Siyo*," he said.

"*'Siyo*," said Thomson. He smiled and nodded. He was glad that a second lawman had seen him with the first, probably assuming them to be friends. Then he continued his way toward Muskogee Avenue, Tahlequah's main street. There were still plenty of people walking around over there. He might see someone he knew, someone to chat with, but that was not really his purpose. It would have been his purpose under ordinary circumstances. But this time he had a plan. He had something to accomplish. He had to find Eli Martin. And he reminded himself that he needed to do so without calling attention to himself and his purpose. He could not afford to go around asking folks if they had seen Martin. He just had to find him on his own.

He walked along Muskogee Avenue, trying his best to appear casual, speaking to a few people along the way, looking at each cluster of men gathered in conversation, until he had taken himself almost out of town. There was nothing more ahead. No place else to look, except, of course, the sale barn.

He called himself thickheaded for not having thought of that immediately. It was the place men gathered to buy and sell livestock, and during the time when the council was in session, they always gathered there because there were so many people in town anyway. It was a place where men could gather together and talk man talk. They could curse and spit and look at cattle and horses and hogs. It was a constant hangout when it was in use, and men would sometimes stay there long into the night. It was also the logical and natural place for Eli Martin to be found.

Thomson thought about going back to his campsite for Old Jeb, but he decided against that. If anyone saw him walk back to his camp and mount up and ride out again, they would assume that he had some definite purpose, and he did not want anyone to make such an assumption. Besides that, it was not really such a long walk. He could manage it easily enough, and Old Jeb had gone a long way that day already. It would be best to leave him alone for a while. He shifted the valise to his other hand and continued walking south.

Chapter

5

Thomson was only about half way to the sale barn when he decided that he'd made a mistake. It was too dark. He was just about to turn around and go back when he saw a faint glimmer of light ahead. A small fire or a lantern, he thought. Someone was still there. Well, he was almost there. He might as well go on.

A few more steps and he could hear faint voices, then a little laughter. Just as he thought. There were still some men hanging around down there, probably talking pigs, he told himself.

The barn was a long but simple pole shed with corrals in front and off to each side. There were holding pens and chutes alongside the corrals, and there was a platform by one fence where the auctioneer could stand up and be seen by the whole crowd, when a crowd was gathered there.

Thomson was walking up behind the barn. The light was in front of the barn, so he lost its glow for the moment. He turned a corner

to walk along beside a fence, and in the darkness he almost walked head on into another
man coming from the other direction.

"Hey," said the other.

"Oh," said Thomson. "Sorry. I didn't see
you coming there. You almost scared the shit
out of me."

"Ah, no harm done," said the other. "Wait
a minute. Is that you, Mr. Matthew
Thomson, you sorry son of a bitch?"

"Martin? Eli Martin?"

"You goddamn right, Thomson."

What luck, thought Thomson. What incredible luck. Everything's going my way. His
heart rate increased with excitement, and he
could feel it race.

"Eli," he said, "I was looking for you. I really
was."

"I'll bet you were."

"No. Really. I came down here to
Tahlequah mainly because I thought you
might be here. I feel bad about the way I done
you in St. Louis, and I want to apologize. I
guess I was just a bit nervous up there in the
city, trying to do business with the big shots.
I'm really sorry for the way I acted."

Martin gave a noncommittal grunt.

"Come on, Eli," pleaded Thomson. "Say,
I've got some real good stuff here that I
brought back with me from St. Louis. Let's
have a few drinks and let bygones be bygones.
What do you say?"

49

"Well, I don't know," said Martin.

Thomson could tell that Martin was weakening, and by this time he had also smelled the whiskey on the cowboy's breath. He knew he had him.

"Come on," he said.

"Well, hell, I ain't never been one to hold no grudges," said Martin, suddenly clapping an arm around Thomson's shoulder. "All right. Let's go."

They walked back around the barn, the way Thomson had come, but they had only gone a few steps when Martin stopped.

"Let's have a taste," he said.

"Right here?" said Thomson.

"Sure. Why not?"

"Those fellows right over there," said Thomson.

"Hell, don't mind them. I know them all. Anyhow, they ain't coming around here. Come on. Let's have it."

Thomson pulled the valise open and felt for the bottles. He had to get the right one, but he could tell by the way in which the bottles were placed. He had been careful about that. He grasped what he was sure was the bottle containing the whiskey, pulled it out of the valise, uncorked it, and took a quick sniff. It was the whiskey. He held it out toward Martin.

"Here you go," he said.

"After you," said Martin. "It's your whiskey."

"That's all right. I've got another one in here." He pulled out the other bottle, the one he had filled with tea. "See? One for you and one for me."

He pulled the cork on the fake bottle and tipped it up to his lips.

"By God," said Martin. "That's all right."

He took a long drink of the whiskey, then shook his head as if to try to clear it.

"Damn. That is good stuff, Matt. That's real Saint Looey whiskey."

He took another drink, and Thomson drank again from his bottle.

"Say," he said, "let's head back toward town. I'd hate to get drunk all the way out here."

They started walking slowly and easily back north, halting every few steps to drink. Things were working out just right, Thomson thought.

"Where you staying in town anyway?" he asked.

"I got a room at the National Hotel," said Martin. "How about you?"

"Aw, I come in late, so I'm camping out on the creek."

"Well, hell, pard, why don't you move on in with me? I got a whole damn room to myself. We'll just about be there when these bottles are empty."

"Thanks, Eli," said Thomson. "I'll have to go down by my campsite, though. I left some stuff down there."

"That's all right. Hell, we'll just go there first."

Thomson noticed that Martin was walking more slowly and weaving a bit. That was good, he thought. He'll be good and drunk by the time we get downtown. Thomson started to weave a bit himself and slur his speech just a little. He wanted Martin to think that he was getting drunk along with him.

By the time they reached the livery stable, both bottles were nearly empty. Thomson had a moment of brief panic. What if Martin finished his bottle first and asked for a drink out of the other? He stopped walking, put the bottle to his lips and leaned back his head, draining the bottle of its tea.

"Ah," he said. "Damn, that was good."

He tossed the bottle to the side of the road with a flourish.

"Well, hell," said Martin. Then he imitated the actions of Thomson, emptying the bottle he carried. He tossed it after the other one.

"There. We done it. It was a tough job, partner, but somebody had to do it."

"Yeah," said Thomson. "Come on. Let's go get my stuff."

Go-Ahead Rider, sheriff of Tahlequah District, sat behind his desk in his office in the Cherokee National Prison, his feet up on the desk, chair back on two legs. His arms

52

were crossed over his chest. The two .36 caliber Navy Colts that he usually carried in the waistband of his trousers were lying on the desk in front of him. It had been a long day, and he was ready to go home to his wife and children, so he was pleased when his deputy, George Tanner, stepped into the office.

"It's real quiet out there now," said George.

"Good. Let's hope it stays that way for a while," said Rider.

"You've got five deputies still over at the capitol."

"Yeah. I was just thinking about them. Why don't you run back over there and round them up. Send everyone home except for Beehunter. He can stand the night watch. You go on home from there. I'll lock this place up."

"Okay."

Tanner started to leave the office, but Rider stopped him.

"Just tell those boys to be sure and be back on the job in the morning," he said.

"I'll tell them."

Rider stood up and stretched as Tanner left the office. There was no one in jail that night, an amazing fact with so many people in town. Rider had expected to have at least a few drunks by this time. Well, he'd just lock up the building and head for the house. On the way, he'd stop by the capitol and visit a little with Beehunter.

He had decided to leave Beehunter on duty because, of all the temporary help he used from time to time, Beehunter was the most reliable. In fact, Rider often wished that he could secure the approval of the council to hire Beehunter full time, but so far they had refused. They couldn't come up with the money, they always said. And what did Rider need with two full-time deputies? And on top of that, Beehunter couldn't even speak English. There were more and more Cherokee citizens who spoke only English and more and more whites being allowed into the Cherokee Nation all the time. It didn't make sense to the council, or to the administration for that matter, to have a deputy who couldn't speak to all the citizens. Of course, it didn't worry them that George couldn't speak to all of the citizens either. Ah well. At least he could give Beehunter all of the temporary hours he could scrape up for him.

Thomson and Martin staggered along Muskogee Avenue. As they were about to pass the jail, or National Prison, Thomson put an arm around Martin's shoulder and guided him off to the right.

"Let's cut across this way," he said. "My camp's just down there."

The path that Thomson had in mind would have taken the two men between the jail and the supreme court building, but as they got close to the jail, Thomson noticed the deputy step out the front door. He let his arm fall off Martin's shoulder, and he slowed his pace, allowing Martin to get ahead. Martin staggered on, unaware.

Thomson bent over and felt around on the ground for a good throwing rock. It didn't take long to find it. For once he was thankful for the rocky soil of the Cherokee Nation. He stood up with the rock in his hand and looked around. Off to his right was a tall tree with a thick trunk. He balanced the rock in his hand, gauged the distance, took aim, and let it fly. Then he quickly ducked behind the tree.

"Ow!"

George Tanner felt the impact of the rock between his shoulder blades. He whirled to look behind him, and he saw the man staggering along alone. There was no one else in sight. The man was not real close, George noticed. He had made a pretty good throw. But George was too mad to praise the culprit. He hurried to meet the man.

"What did you mean by that?" he demanded.

"What?" said Martin. "What you talking about?"

"You know what I'm talking about. Besides that, you're drunk. Come along with me."

"I'm not drunk," said Martin, his speech slurred almost beyond understanding.

George took him by the arm and pulled him toward the front door of the jail.

"Come on," he said. Martin allowed himself to be dragged along. He was too far gone to do otherwise. When George got back to the door with his prisoner, Rider was just about to come out.

"Looks like we spoke too soon," he said.

"Yeah," said George. "Well, he's not only drunk, he heaved a rock and hit me right in the middle of my back."

"You hurt?" Rider asked.

"I've probably got a pretty good bruise."

"Well, put him in a cell," said Rider. "That kind of changes our plans just a little bit, don't it? You wait here while I go see the boys. Be right back."

Rider couldn't leave a prisoner in a cell overnight with no one in the jail. It was a policy, and one that Rider agreed with. It was partly to guard the prisoner and partly for the prisoner's own protection. A man could get sick, or he might try to hurt himself. Someone in a responsible position had to stay around. He walked across to the capitol square and rounded up the five temporary deputies.

"Beehunter," he said, speaking in the Cherokee language, "can you stay on duty all night?"

"Yes, I can," the deputy said.

"I have a prisoner in the jail, and I need a

deputy to spend the night there. Okay?"

"Okay."

"Good. Go on over there now. George is there, and I'll be on over soon."

Beehunter took off for the jail at a trot, and Rider turned to the others and shifted to English.

"You fellows can all go home but one of you," he said. "That's all I need for the night. Just one. Does it matter much to you who stays?"

No one said anything for a moment, so finally Earl Bob spoke up.

"I'll stay if nobody else wants to," he said.

He glanced at the others, and so did Rider, but no one spoke.

"Okay," said Rider. "That's fine then, but I want the rest of you back here in the morning first thing. Y'all know the routine."

"Yeah," said Delbert Swim. "We'll be here. Good night, Go-Ahead."

"Good night, boys," said Rider. He walked back to the jail and went inside. George and Beehunter were sitting in chairs in the office staring at the floor. George could speak no Cherokee and Beehunter no English. They always seemed just a little awkward around each other, and that always amused Rider just a little.

"Beehunter's going to stay the night, George," the sheriff said as he walked in. "You can go on home now. Get your pretty young wife to rub that sore back."

George's face turned slightly red as he headed for the door.

"Yeah," he said. "Good night."

Rider reverted to Cherokee again as soon as George was gone.

"Come with me," he said. "Let's see where George put the prisoner."

"He showed me already," said Beehunter. "He's upstairs on the east side. Middle cell."

"Okay," said Rider. "Is he awake?"

"Passed out."

"Well, he probably won't give you any trouble then. You can go back in the sleeping room and use the cot. But first, after I leave, be sure all the doors are locked so no one can come in. Make coffee if you want it. Sleep if you want unless something happens. You know where to get me if you need me."

Matt Thomson watched from the dark cover behind the tree as Rider left the jail. His heart was pounding, loudly, he thought. But he smiled. So far everything had worked out perfectly.

Chapter
6

Thomson could scarcely believe his good luck, finding Martin so easily on the first night and then coming up by the jail just as the deputy was stepping out the door. But it hadn't all been luck, he reminded himself. He had planned everything very carefully, and so far his plan was working perfectly. And part of it was due to his quick thinking, he boasted to himself silently. He hadn't really known just exactly how he was going to get Martin thrown into jail. He had thought that he might somehow get the man into a fight with someone. But throwing the rock at that deputy — that had been a stroke of pure genius.

He was excited and wanted to hurry on through the rest of his plan, but he deliberately slowed himself down. Stay calm, he said to himself. You have all night. He noticed that there were still a few people walking along Muskogee Avenue. Soon the town would be asleep though. He told himself that he might as well go back to his camp and get a little sleep. He was glad that he had drunk the bottle of tea. He would lie down on his bedroll without bothering to relieve himself first, and the pressure on his bladder would wake him up after he'd had a short nap. That would make the timing just about right, he figured.

Go-Ahead Rider walked up to the top of the bluff that overlooked Tahlequah and on north just a little to his house. Really it was two log cabins with a dog run between them. As he approached the door, it was opened from the inside by his wife. He stepped in and put his arms around her.

"Exie," he said, talking Cherokee, "you don't have to wait up for me."

He had known, of course, that she would. She always did when he was late.

"I know," she said. "I wanted to wait for you."

"Are the kids asleep?"

"Yes. For about an hour already."

"I don't like to get home so late," he said, "after they're in bed. But it's only when the council's meeting."

"Did you have any trouble today?"

"Just when we were ready to lock everything up and go home," said Rider, "a drunk hit George with a rock. Right outside of the jail, too."

"Oh. Is George all right?"

"He's all right. The drunk's in jail passed

out, and Beehunter's staying the night in the office."

"Are you hungry? You want anything?"

"I only want you," said Rider. "Let's go to bed."

Thomson woke up with a powerful urge to urinate. He got up and looked around. No one seemed to be stirring anywhere. He walked behind a tree to relieve himself, then, heaving a long sigh, he walked back to his bedroll. He picked up his valise in one hand, felt around for the cane pole, found it, and picked it up in the other. Looking around again, he started walking toward the jail.

The bluff that overlooked Tahlequah was on the east side of Wolfe Creek. On the west side of the creek ran Water Street. The campers were between the creek and the street. The main part of Tahlequah was west of Water Street, with the capitol square the focal point and center of the town. South of the capitol was the supreme court building and south of that the jail.

It was along Water Street that Thomson walked. When he found himself just east of the jail, he moved closer to the creek and hid himself in under the trees. He put the cane pole on the ground in front of him and then opened the valise. He felt around for the pocket pistol and then for the bullet. He took them out of the valise.

Then taking the Rupertus pistol in his right hand he set the hammer at half cock and with his left hand rotated the barrel. He inserted the bullet, then twisted the barrel back into place. He felt around inside the valise again until he found the roll of twine that had been his fishing line. He took it out and unrolled a length of it.

He took up the smallest end of the cane pole and lined up the barrel of the pistol with the pole, the end of the barrel just about even with the end of the pole, and then he wrapped the twine around and around tightly, securing the pistol firmly to the pole. When he was satisfied with the wrapping, he tied the string, pulled a penknife out of his pocket, and cut off the excess.

Next came the tricky part. He found the piece of rawhide thong and tied it in a small loop around the stud trigger, almost but not quite tight. He picked up an end of the excess line and tied it to the loop. Then he threaded the other end of the long line through the eyelets along the pole clear back to the opposite end. He was almost done.

Carefully he pulled the hammer back to full cock, and he realized that he was sweating. He told himself that it was a warm night, wiped his brow on his shirt sleeve and reached back into the valise for the buffalo-hide mitten. He held the mitten in his left hand and stuffed the pistol, muzzle first, into the mitten. It was all ready.

He stood up and picked up the pole by the thick end, the end opposite the pistol. The pole bowed a little from the weight of the pistol, but not much, and if he moved slowly, he could maneuver it around without causing it to wave out of control. It would work. He knew it would. It had to. He was too far into this now, he thought, to back out, and there was too much at stake. He had his fortune to make.

He took the pole in the middle and stepped out of his hiding place. He could see no signs of life. He hurried across Water Street to the National Prison, looked around once more, then ran up to press himself against the east wall of the jail. There were cells on both levels of the building. Where the hell, he wondered, had they put Martin?

The lower level of the building was half underground so that the cell windows were at ground level. The windows of the second floor cells were too high up from the ground for even a tall man to look into. He hoped that Martin was in a ground-floor cell, but even more, he hoped that he had been put in a cell with a window.

He bent over to look through the bars of the window nearest him, that at the northeast corner on the front, and he suffered his next moment of panic. It was dark inside, almost too dark to see anything. He squinted his eyes and strained to see. Finally he thought that he could make out the outline of the cot against the wall, and he thought that no one was lying on it. But he wasn't sure. He moved on to the next window anyway.

When he had worked his way all around the building and looked in each of the ground-level windows, he had still not seen any sign of anyone until he looked in at the office windows at the northwest corner of the building. A lantern burned in the front office. It was turned down low, but it gave out enough light for Thomson to see that no one was in the office. There was a door in the office that led to another room, and that door was open. Enough light spilled into that room to allow Thomson to see on through.

In that room adjacent to the office, Thomson could see, a man was asleep on a cot, but clearly it was not Martin. He could tell that at a glance. The man appeared to be a full-blooded Indian, and he was armed. Anyhow, the room was not a cell. It must be the deputy on duty.

Damn, he thought. They've put Martin on the second floor or in a cell without a window. For a moment he thought that all of his careful planning had gone for naught, but he refused to give it up so easily. It was still the middle of the night. There was still no sign of life in the streets, and he still had time. He walked back around to the west side of the building and carefully placed his cane pole down on the ground close to the wall. Even if someone came by, he would never notice it there in the dark.

He hurried across Water Street and picked up his valise from the bushes, then walked fast back to his campsite. He put the valise down beside his blanket, picked up the saddle and saddle blanket, and moved to the side of Old Jeb.

"How you doing there, old boy?" he said, speaking in a low and soothing voice. "You doing all right? Good. That's a good old boy, Jeb."

As he talked, he stroked the animal's head and neck. Then he rubbed his back.

"We going to go for a little ride, old boy," he said, and he threw the blanket on the horse's back. "How's that?" he said. "Okay?" He tossed on the saddle. He was being careful not to do anything to wake up his neighbors, and Old Jeb cooperated. It seemed to Thomson almost as if the horse understood his needs, if not his purpose. Ready at last, he led Old Jeb slowly out onto Water Street, then mounted up and rode casually back to the jail.

Once more, Thomson looked up and down the streets for any sign of life and saw none. Tahlequah was asleep. He eased on up into the jail yard, dismounted, and picked up the cane pole. Then he climbed back into the saddle and rode up to the window in the middle of the west wall. Some clouds rolled overhead and the moon suddenly shed some light from its position in the western sky.

That's good if Martin's on this side of the building, Thomson said to himself, but only if nobody else comes along. Now anybody could see me real good, too. He patted Old Jeb on the neck.

"Hold still, old boy," he said. "Real still. That's right. Just hold it there now."

He had walked Old Jeb up as close to the wall as he could get him, his right side against the wall. Holding the pole in the middle in his right hand, he placed it against the wall to brace himself. Then he slipped his left foot out of the stirrup and stepped up onto the saddle. When his left foot was firmly planted, he brought up his right.

Standing on Old Jeb's back and with the bright moon over his shoulder, Thomson could see clearly into the dark, second-floor cell. There was Martin, flat on his back on the cot and out cold. Thomson told himself that his luck had returned.

The cot was to Thomson's right as he looked in through the bars, and Martin's head was toward the outside wall. Thomson thought for a second about the angle of the shot. It should not appear to have come from outside. He pushed the pole, pistol first, through the bars, until the entire pole was inside the cell, and both of his arms were almost all inside.

Carefully he turned the pole, holding it parallel to the outside wall, and tilted it, lowering the pistol until its muzzle was actually touching the chest of Eli Martin. He waited a moment to see if Martin would react. He did not. He was totally passed out. Thomson pressed the muzzle against Martin a little harder. Then he grasped the string and pulled.

The sound it made through the heavy mitten was more of a *poof* than a bang, and the man in the cell only gave a slight twitch. He made no sound, and he moved no more. It had all worked even better than Thomson had thought it would.

His heart pounding, he worked the pole around and pulled it back out through the bars. Then he dropped back down into the saddle and turned Old Jeb to ride back to his camp. He had to hold himself back, to check the impulse to really put the spurs to Old Jeb, and he did. He managed it. He rode slowly, casually, to his spot beside the creek.

Once there, he unsaddled Old Jeb and in a low voice praised him highly while stroking his back and neck. Then he moved back to his blanket on the ground, took out his penknife, and cut the strings that bound the pistol to the pole. He put the pistol back into the valise and tossed the pole on the ground.

It was done. It was perfect. No one would ever figure it out.

A cane pole is just that, he said to himself. A fishing pole. They're all over the place. It wouldn't mean anything to anyone. And the pistol? Hell, everyone had one of them, too. He'd leave it in the valise and take it on home with him later. So that's it. Except for the mitten. Panic returned. Where was the mitten? The mitten that had been used to muffle the shot and that now had a bullet hole in its end.

He looked all around on the ground. It was nowhere to be seen. "God damn," he said in a harsh whisper. He stood up and started retracing his route back to the jail, walking with his head down, looking all around. By the time he found himself once again just across the road from the jail, he had still not seen the mitten.

His heart pounded embarrassingly in his chest. He did not want to walk back across the road, back into the jail yard, back up to the wall right there where he had done the deed. He had heard that criminals always returned to the scene of the crime, and that was one of the reasons they usually got caught. He did not want to make that mistake. But then, he did not want to leave any evidence behind him either. Where was the damn mitten?

He stood in the tall weeds at the edge of

the woods on the creek side of Water Street and stared across at the jail. He looked up and down the street and all around, and still he could see no sign of life in the sleeping town. He crossed the street and walked back to the east wall underneath the window to the cell. Still he saw no mitten.

He walked back to his campsite and sat down on his bedroll to think. It doesn't matter, he told himself. If I couldn't find it, probably they won't either. And even if they do, how would they connect it with the shooting of the man in the cell? They won't, of course.

He decided that he had panicked over nothing. He was trying to be too careful. His scheme was so clever, he told himself, that even if they had the cane pole and the line and the mitten, they would never figure out what he had done with them. And if by some miracle they did figure out that much, there was no way they would be able to find out who had done it. He relaxed again, and he stretched out on the bedroll with a smug smile on his face.

Chapter
7

Rider was up early the next morning. With the council in session, five extra deputies on duty, all the people in town from all over the Nation, and the illegal booze that he knew was flowing, he anticipated a long and tiring day. He was dressed and ready to go by the time Exie had their breakfast ready. Then the two Rider children got up. Tootie and her little brother Buster wanted to have breakfast with their daddy before he left for the day. They were sleepy eyed, but they already knew that their mother would probably put them to bed again that night before he would make it home from work.

Rider stayed at the table for as long as he felt he could, then, "I've got to go, kids," he said. He stood up and went to the hat rack for his hat.

"Will you be late again tonight?" asked Buster. "Like last night?"

"I don't know, *chooj*," said Rider. "I'll come home as soon as I can, though. That's a promise. Okay?"

"Well, I guess so," said Buster. "We'll wait up for you, though, if Mama will let us."

"You mind your mama," said Rider. "If she says it's okay, you can wait up, but if she tells you to go to bed, you do what she says. You hear?"

"Yes," said Buster.

"We always do," said Tootie. "Don't worry, Daddy."

Rider kissed Exie and Tootie and shook hands with Buster to make him feel big. Then he left the house to walk down to the jail.

George Tanner knocked on the front door of the National Prison.

"Wake up. Wake up," he shouted. "It's morning. Time to go to work."

He knocked again, and, in a lower voice than before, he said, "You can't even understand a word I'm saying, can you? Ah, I should have taken a little more time and let Rider get here first."

Then he heard the sound of the latch sliding, and the door was pulled open from the inside. Beehunter stood there rubbing his eyes with the back of his hand.

" '*Siyo*, Jaji," he said.

" '*Siyo*," said George, nearly exhausting his Cherokee vocabulary. He felt a little self-conscious about using even that one word. He was never quite sure he was pronouncing

71

it correctly. He pushed himself on past Beehunter, almost rudely, he realized, and went on into the office. He picked up the coffeepot and saw right away that it was still cold. He put it back on the stove top with a clank as Beehunter came back in.

"Kawis jaduli?" said Beehunter.

"Huh? Yeah. Yeah," said George. *"Kawi.* Yeah. And while you're doing that, I'll just go up and take a look at the prisoner."

Beehunter gave Tanner an inquisitive look.

"Prisoner. Prisoner," said Tanner, pointing toward the upstairs cells. Beehunter nodded, as if he finally understood, and George left the office. He walked up the stairs and along the line of cells until he reached the middle one, where he had deposited the drunken prisoner the night before. The man was lying on his back on the cot. George could still feel the bruise from the rock, and he was still angry at the man who had thrown it. He was anxious for a chance to challenge the man after he had sobered up, to ask him why he had done such a stupid thing.

"Hey, you," he said. "Wake up."

The man did not move. Then George realized that something was wrong. He looked more closely. Blood. Was that blood? On the man's chest and on the floor beneath the cot. Blood. He turned and ran back downstairs to the office and around behind Rider's desk. He jerked open a desk drawer and pulled out the big key ring. Beehunter was stoking up the fire in the stove in order to boil water for coffee.

"Get Rider," said George. "Rider."

Though Beehunter did not understand English, he had heard Rider called by his name in English often enough to recognize that word. He shut the stove door and straightened up. George was already out the office door and half way up the stairs again. Beehunter looked after him, perplexed.

"Doyust guhsti?" he said.

George did not slow down, but he shouted to Beehunter as he continued on his way back to the cell.

"I don't know what the hell you're saying. Just go get Rider. Get Rider."

Beehunter understood that something was wrong and that George kept saying "Rider." He went to the front door and opened it again, went outside and started toward Rider's house. He had gone only a few steps away from the jail when he saw Rider coming. He hurried ahead to meet him.

"Rider," he said in Cherokee, "Jaji says come fast."

"What's wrong?" said Rider.

"I don't know. He just yelled at me. 'Rider. Rider.' He was upstairs at the cell where the prisoner is kept."

"Did you see the prisoner this morning?"

"No. I just got up. Jaji came in and went

73

upstairs. Then he started yelling at me."

"Well," Rider said, "let's go see what's bothering him."

They found George upstairs in the cell, standing beside the cot, looking down at the body lying there, a grim expression on his face. He looked almost as if he might be sick.

"It looks like he's been shot, Rider," he said.

"Yeah," said Rider, stepping into the cell, "and from real close range, too, I'd say. That looks like powder burns on his shirt there, don't it? Looks like the gun was pushed right up against his chest. You find the cell open like this when you come up here?"

"No, sir," said George. "It was locked up tight. When I saw that the man was shot, I ran back down to get the keys."

Rider dropped down on one knee close to the cot, and he leaned over to get a look underneath. Then straightening up again, but still on his knee, he looked more closely at the entrance wound on the chest.

"What's this here?" he said, and he carefully plucked some fur from around the wound. He turned to Beehunter and held the fur out toward him. *"Gadousdi hia?"* he said.

Beehunter took the fur and looked at it closely.

"Yansa," he said.

"What'd he say?" asked George.

"Buffalo," said Rider. "It's buffalo fur." Then as if musing to himself, he repeated, "Buffalo fur and powder burns." Then he stood up and sighed.

"George," he said, "run over to the capitol and see the judge. Get the right papers from him to have this body taken care of. You can tell him everything you know, which I gather ain't much. I'll be here talking to Beehunter."

"Rider," said George.

"Run on, George," said Rider. "We'll have plenty of time to talk this all out."

"Yes, sir."

George headed for the stairway. For the next moment or two, Rider and Beehunter were silent there in the cell with the bloody body.

"Do you know him?" Rider asked, speaking Cherokee, and gesturing toward the cot with his head.

"I've seen him in town," Beehunter answered. "Mostly down at the sale barn, I think."

"Did you hear a shot during the night?"

"No. I slept. Nothing woke me up. I think I would have heard a shot, though. I don't understand this, Rider."

"I don't either. Did you let anyone in the building any time during the night?"

"No. No one. When you left, I locked the doors. Bolted them from inside. I didn't open a door until Jaji knocked this morning."

"Did you check on the prisoner any time during the night?"

"He was passed out, and he never made a noise, so I just left him alone. Rider, how could this happen? Through the window?"

"Right now I can't see how," said Rider. "You go on downstairs and have a cup of coffee. I'll be down in a minute or two."

Beehunter did as Rider said, and Rider squatted down beside the cot. Again he looked underneath. He estimated the angle of the trajectory of the bullet, as well as the direction from which the shot had come, by the positions of the entrance and exit wounds. Then he stood up and stared at the cell wall opposite the cot. He shook his head.

"No," he said, talking to himself out loud in English, "that angle don't matter none. The gun was pressed right against his chest."

The powder burns on the shirt indicated that much, and so did the fact that the bullet had gone all the way through the body and the cot beneath it. The bullet, Rider thought. It must be on the floor. Again he knelt down and looked under the cot. He followed the angle of the shot and saw where the bullet had nicked the cement floor. Then he spotted it in the corner against the outside wall. He stretched his arm underneath the cot, being careful not to drag his sleeve through the puddle of nearly dried blood on the floor, and he picked up the bullet. Then he stood up and walked downstairs to the office.

Beehunter was sitting calmly in a straight-backed chair against a bare space of wall. He had a cup of coffee in his hand.

"Here's the bullet," said Rider, again speaking Cherokee. He laid it on the top of his desk. "You still have that little fluff of buffalo hair I handed you upstairs?"

Beehunter held a hand out toward Rider, and Rider took the bit of fur from him. He placed that on his desk beside the bullet.

"Beehunter," he said, "you know what this looks like, don't you?"

"It looks bad for me," said the deputy.

"Well, you didn't kill the man, did you?"

"No."

"That's good enough for me," said Rider, "but then here's what we have. It looks like the building was locked up tight. You were down here asleep. The prisoner was locked in his cell and passed out on the cot. Someone stood inside the cell, pressed a gun against the prisoner's chest and fired a shot, killing him, and the shot didn't make enough noise to disturb you. That's what we've got to work with. That and a little bit of buffalo fur."

Beehunter said nothing in response, but Rider already knew what Beehunter must be thinking. Since there did not appear to be any rational explanation for what had happened to the yet unidentified prisoner, Beehunter was almost certainly thinking that the only possible reason was something other than rational. He was thinking that either the prisoner or he, himself, or both were victims of some kind of witchcraft.

Rider almost admitted to himself that he, too, was considering that possibility, but he couldn't proceed on that basis. His job said that he had to pursue the logical, plausible, rational explanation as far as it could possibly take him.

Yet Go-Ahead Rider was faced with a major dilemma. He believed Beehunter. There was no question about that. He would trust Beehunter with his life. In fact, in the past, more than once, he had done exactly that. And Beehunter had said that the building had stayed locked all night and that he had heard no shot.

The evidence in the cell all indicated that the man had been shot at close range, with the weapon, in fact, pressed right up against his chest. The physical evidence and Beehunter's assertions did not fit together.

Rider told himself then that if the physical evidence and Beehunter's claims were so contradictory as to indicate that one of them must be lying, he would have to say then that the physical evidence was the liar. And if physical evidence lied, that was a strong indication of witchcraft. But could it indicate anything else?

Yes, he told himself. It could indicate that someone had somehow manipulated the physical evidence to make it appear that one thing had happened when in reality something very different had taken place.

Then Rider's path became clear. Beehunter was telling the truth, and so Rider's job was going to be to figure out how the physical evidence had been tampered with and why and by whom.

Only two things were possible, it seemed. Someone had to have killed the prisoner from outside the building, finding some way to make it look as if the job had been done on the inside, or someone had to have found a way to get into and out of a locked building and a locked cell without having been detected by the deputy who slept in the room adjacent to the office. One of those two things, but which one?

While Rider was puzzling over these things, George Tanner came back into the office with some papers in his hand.

"The judge is coming over for a look," he said. "He's not very happy about this."

"Nobody is, George," said Rider.

"And they'll be along in a few minutes to take the body out of here."

"When they come for it, George, I want to be sure and tell them that I want that shirt. In fact, I want you and me and Beehunter to go into the cell with them, and the judge, too, if he's still around, and I want to figure out the angle of the shot with witnesses there. I want plenty of witnesses for all the physical evidence that'll get messed up when the body's moved. You understand me?"

"Yes, sir, I do," said George. "Anything else?"

"No, George. Nothing more for now. Not until they've come and gone. Just sit down and relax. I'm going to walk around the building some. Yell at me when the judge gets here."

Chapter
8

The morning after the killing, Thomson had a powerful urge to get out of Tahlequah, to hurry back to the security of his own home up north in the Delaware District. He told himself that he needed to get back to take care of business, that his partner barely had the sense to load the merchandise at the station in Seneca and get it delivered to his own property and unloaded into the warehouse barn. He had a feeling that if the local laws in Tahlequah saw him, they would see guilt in his face, and so he should get his face far beyond their sight. He had lost the mitten, and though he had told himself that it was not important, it still bothered him. He had all of those thoughts and feelings, and then he fought them all off.

He would not act like a guilty man. He was a Cherokee citizen interested in the politics of his nation. He had even run for a council position once. It was normal and natural for him to be in the capital city when the council was in session.

He reminded himself of how carefully he

had planned and executed the killing of Eli Martin. There was no way that anyone would ever be able to connect him to the deed. He imagined the puzzled, even befuddled, laws trying to figure out what had happened. He had heard of Go-Ahead Rider, of course. He guessed that everyone in the Cherokee Nation knew about Rider; a hero of the Civil War, Rider had been a captain in the Indian Home Guard fighting on the side of the union. Since the war, Rider had become known as a fearless officer of the law. It did Thomson's heart good to think about Rider trying to figure this one out. He decided to stay and watch.

There was one problem, though. He pulled all of the money out of his pockets and counted it, and there just wasn't much left. After he'd paid for his meals for the day, he'd be damn near broke. He decided that he would have to go right into his new business, and he knew just where to go to get his start.

Hoak Fletcher had a cabin just outside of Tahlequah by the river, and if Thomson couldn't find Hoak in town, he would surely be able to find him at home. He decided to pack everything up there at his campsite. He didn't really want to spend another night on the ground anyway. Martin had said that he had a room at the National Hotel. Thomson saddled Old Jeb, picked up his valise, and rode to the hotel.

"I was just wondering if anything's opened up since last night," Thomson said to the desk clerk.

"Funny you should ask that," said the clerk. "Man in number seven never showed after he checked in. He only paid for the night, and the night's over. You can have his room if you want it."

"Well, I don't know," said Thomson. "Did he leave his stuff in the room?"

"He never put nothing in it to start with. Came in here and paid for the night and then went right back out. He never came back at all. Never went up to the room. He didn't even pick up a key."

"I'll take it," said Thomson, "and I will take the key."

He paid for the room, and then he was broke, but he took his valise and his blanket roll upstairs. Then he went back out, mounted Old Jeb and started to ride along Muskogee Avenue. His plan was to look the town over for any sign of Hoak Fletcher. If he couldn't find him that way, he'd ride out to the river.

And Thomson's luck held. He looked in three different public eating houses, and in the third one, there sat Hoak. Thomson left Old Jeb tied outside and went in and over to Hoak's table. Hoak was alone and eating a big breakfast. Thomson tried to ignore the growling in his stomach as he pulled out a chair. He hoped that Hoak wouldn't be able to hear it.

"Howdy, Hoak," he said. "Do you mind?"

"Naw. Sit down," said Hoak. "What's been going on?"

"You remember that deal I talked to you about a while back?"

Hoak looked up from his meal and stared into Thomson's eyes for a moment. Then he spoke in a low voice.

"You mean about you running good booze in here? That deal?"

Thomson looked nervously over his shoulder.

"Watch what you're saying, Hoak, damn it."

"Ah, hell, nobody heard me. Is that what you're talking about?"

"Yeah. That. Are you still interested? Seriously?"

"I said I was. Sure."

"I've got the merchandise, but you've got to pay me here and then pick it up at my partner's place."

"You didn't say nothing about no partner."

"My neighbor across the line. You know him. Joe Carter."

"Oh, yeah. I know Joe."

"Well, Joe's barn is our warehouse. We got a whole shipment today, and Joe loaded it in. It's safe over there. It's legal, you know?"

"Yeah?"

"Well, here's the deal. You pay me now for

however much you want, and I write you out a note for Joe. Take the note up there and he'll give you the stuff. You want it? You can double your money."

Thomson felt much better with money in his pockets again. After getting the payment from Hoak and giving Hoak the promised note, he left the eating establishment. As hungry as he was, he didn't want Hoak or anyone else to know that he had been broke. It wouldn't have looked right, he thought, if he had taken Hoak's money and right away ordered something to eat.

He rode back to the livery stable and offered the man there double his usual fee if he could find a way to board Old Jeb, and the man took it. Thomson strolled away from the livery feeling very puffed up. That's the way it goes, he told himself, when a man's got money. Just anything you want. Anything at all. No room, you say? Just wave enough money under his nose, and he'll find the room.

He was walking back toward the capitol building when he found himself even with the National Prison, and he couldn't have said exactly why he did it, but he walked on over there and went inside. Go-Ahead Rider was sitting behind his desk. Just across the desk from Rider, George Tanner was standing. Beehunter was sitting in the chair against the wall.

"Excuse me," said Thomson. "Am I interrupting something here?"

"That's all right," said Rider. "I'll be with you in just a minute." He turned his attention back to his deputy. "Just judging by the man's clothes, George," he said, "I'd say go on down to the sale barn and ask around. See if anybody down there might know who he was, and if you get a bite, bring the fellow in to see if he can identify the body."

"Okay, Rider," said George. He picked his hat off the rack and headed for the door.

"George," said Rider.

"Yes, sir?"

"Get yourself a horse out of the barn."

"Yes, sir."

George left the office, and Thomson stepped forward, holding out his hand.

"Excuse me just a minute," said Rider, and he turned to Beehunter and spoke in Cherokee. "You go on home for now," he said. "I'll be in touch with you later."

"Are you sure?" asked Beehunter.

"Go on. I know where to find you if I want you."

"All right," said Beehunter. "I'm going now."

He left, and Rider turned back to Thomson.

"Now," he said, shifting back to English, "what can I do for you?"

"Oh, nothing really," said Thomson. "I just wanted to stop by and meet you. You're the famous Go-Ahead Rider, I guess."

"I'm Rider. Who're you?"

"I'm Matthew Thomson from up in Delaware District. You know, I ran for a council seat from up there the last election. Almost made it. Next time I will. That'll kind of make me your boss, I reckon."

"I reckon," said Rider. "If you win."

"I'm in town because of the council meeting," said Thomson. "I like to keep up with things. My interest in politics and all, you know."

"Yeah."

"You have some trouble here? I'm not trying to be nosey, just interested. I heard you say something about needing to identify somebody. It sounded like you was talking about a corpse. You said 'who he was.' "

"I did say that, didn't I?" said Rider. "Well, the talk'll be all over town before the day's out. We had a prisoner in here last night. Drunk. He was killed in the cell."

"Inside the jail?" said Thomson.

"That's what it looks like."

"At night inside the jail?"

"Yeah."

"Well, wasn't anybody here with him? I mean, you or one of your deputies?"

"There was a deputy here," said Rider.

"All night?"

"Yeah."

"You mean he just let somebody walk in here and shoot a prisoner in his cell?"

"Well, I wouldn't put it exactly like that, Mr. Thomson," said Rider. "We're still investigating."

"But if the building was locked up, the prisoner locked inside his cell and no one here but the deputy, and the prisoner was killed in his cell, either the deputy let somebody in, or the deputy did it. Right?"

"We're still investigating, Mr. Thomson. We don't know yet what happened in here last night. We don't even know who the dead man is."

"Yeah," said Thomson. "Sure. I'm sure that you'll handle everything all right. I didn't mean to sound critical. I'm just interested, that's all. Well, I'd better get out of your hair and let you get back to work. I didn't mean to be a bother."

"No bother, Mr. Thomson. You staying in town for the whole council session?"

"I don't know yet. I probably will, though. I'm interested in what goes on with the government, you know."

"Yeah. You said that. You got a hotel room?"

"I'm staying at the National. Maybe I'll see you again before I leave town, Sheriff Rider. Good meeting you."

"Likewise, Mr. Thomson. Have a nice stay in Tahlequah."

"Thank you, and, uh, good luck with your little problem here."

The door opened from the outside, and Judge Harm Boley stepped in, almost walking into Thomson.

"Oh, excuse me," said the judge.

"Excuse me, sir," said Thomson. "I was just leaving."

Thomson left and Boley shut the office door.

"Rider," he said, "what happened in here last night?"

"Didn't George tell you?"

"You tell me again."

"We had a prisoner in one of the upstairs cells. A drunk. He hit George with a rock last night just as we were locking up to go home. When George put him in the cell, he passed right out. We still don't even know who he was, much less who had a reason to kill him."

"Unidentified," said Boley.

"Yeah. Well, Beehunter stayed in here last night. The place was all locked up. Sometime during the night, someone shot the prisoner in the chest. One shot. Killed him."

"What did Beehunter do when he heard the shot?"

"He never heard it."

"Well, where'd the shot come from? Can you tell?"

Rider sighed. He wished the politicians would leave him alone to figure things out instead of wasting his time with their questions.

"It looks like someone held a gun right up

against his chest and shot him," he said.

"What cell is he in?"

"Upstairs."

"I think Tanner told me that the body was lying on its back on the cot. Like he was asleep."

"That's right, Harm," said Rider.

"No one could have held a gun against his chest through the window. Not one of those outside windows. Not even if the man was standing up. And if he was standing up, he wouldn't have fell down on the cot like he was asleep."

"No, sir. I don't reckon he would have."

"Where's Beehunter?"

"I sent him home just a little while ago," said Rider.

"You what?"

"I sent him home."

"Rider, don't you know what this looks like? The building was locked up. Beehunter was the only person in here besides the victim, and he claims that he didn't even hear the shot. That just isn't possible. Why isn't Beehunter under arrest?"

"Harm, Beehunter's at home where I know I can find him if I want him. He told me that the building was locked, and that he didn't let no one in or out all night, and he told me that he didn't hear no shot. I don't know what happened in here last night, but I believe Beehunter, and one way or another,

I'm going to get to the bottom of this."

"Let's go upstairs, Rider," said Boley. "I want to see this for myself."

"Right this way, your honor," said Rider, and he led the way upstairs to the death cell.

Thomson walked along Muskogee Avenue feeling pretty good about himself. He had actually confronted Go-Ahead Rider right there in the man's own office, in the very building in which he had committed the murder, and Rider was in no way suspicious of him. Rider did not know who Martin was and did not know Thomson until he had introduced himself. And while he had been in the office, Thomson had seen no sign of the missing mitten, and the sheriff had given no indication of having gathered any evidence. On the contrary, he had seemed to be completely perplexed by the whole thing. That was just as Thomson had planned, and it made him feel good.

Chapter 9

George Tanner and another man on horseback rode up to the front of the jail and tied their horses. A small gray dog of undetermined breed barked and nipped at the horses' heels. George opened the door and called out.

"Rider. Rider, you in here?"

"Upstairs, George. Come on up."

"Go on," said George to the dog. Then he turned to his companion. "Come on in, Riley," he said.

Riley kicked at the dog and followed George into the building. He pulled the door shut behind him, then the two men climbed the stairs and walked down the hallway to the middle cell. The body was still lying there on the cot. Rider and Judge Boley stood inside the cell. The judge looked terribly upset. Rider looked as he always did.

"Hello, Judge," said George. "Rider, Judge Boley, this is Riley Sam. I met him down at the sale barn."

" '*Siyo*, Riley," said Rider. "How you doing?"

"Just fine, Go-Ahead. You okay?"

"Well, we've got ourselves a little problem here."

"Yeah, I can see that."

"You two know each other, I guess," said George.

"Yeah," said Rider. "Riley, you know Judge Boley here?"

"No, not personal. How do you do, Judge?"

"Glad to meet you, Mr. Sam."

"Rider," said George, "Riley here said that he thought he recognized the description I gave him of our victim."

Riley Sam was by this time staring at the body on the cot. He was shaking his head slowly.

"That's Eli, all right," he said.

"Eli?" said Boley.

"Eli Martin," said Riley Sam. "That's his name. I can't hardly believe this. I was talking to him just last night."

"Down at the sale barn?" asked Rider.

"Yeah. That's right."

"When did you last see him?"

"Oh, I ain't rightly sure, Rider. It was well after dark. Some of us was just hanging out down there, you know, talking late. He left just a few minutes before I did, but I don't know what time it was."

"Do you know where he was going?"

"Well, he walked off like he was headed back this way, you know, into town. I guess he come on in here. I didn't see him again."

"And you don't know what time it was?"

"No, but I remember now I think about it that when I got in town I was going by here, right out there, you know, and I just seen you leaving here, on your way home, I guess."

George gave Rider a look.

"Rider," he said, "that means that Martin came straight here from the sale barn. If he was walking, and Riley here left just a few minutes later on horseback and saw you leave, Martin had to have come straight here, because I already had him in a cell by then, by the time you left."

"Riley," said Rider, "were y'all drinking down there by the barn?"

"No, sir, Rider. I don't drink. You know that."

"Was Martin drinking?"

"Well, he wasn't drinking down there. Nobody had anything to drink, but I do remember thinking that he seemed kind of like he'd had a little, you know?"

"Just a little?"

"Well, he didn't seem too bad to me."

"This might be important, Riley," said Rider. "When George put him in the cell last night, he was staggering drunk, and right away he passed out cold. You say he didn't seem too bad?"

"No. He wasn't drunk like that. Not when I seen him last."

Rider sat behind his desk. In front of him

94

were his own two pistols, the lead from the cell floor, the bit of buffalo fur, and the powder-burned shirt from the dead man's body. The body had at last been removed from the cell. George Tanner sat across the room at the smaller desk.

"George," said Rider, "how did Martin get so drunk between the sale barn and the jailhouse?"

"I don't know, Rider," said George. "Maybe he had something stashed somewhere along the way. Anyhow, I don't really see what difference it makes. When and how he got drunk doesn't have anything to do with the way he was killed."

"Don't be too sure about that, George. We got ourselves several puzzles here, all having to do with that same man last night. Seems to me we got to solve them all to get at the truth."

"It seems to me," said George, "that the truth's pretty obvious. You just aren't ready to admit it. The only thing I don't know is why he did it."

Rider's jaws tightened, but otherwise he showed no outward signs of irritation at what George had just said.

"I want you to ride out to the sale barn, George. Talk to everybody you see there. Find out anything you can about Eli Martin."

George stood up and went for his hat. With a slight scowl, he pulled the hat down tight on his head.

"Yes, sir," he said.

"And George."

"Yes?"

"On the way out, take your time. Poke around. See what you can see along the way."

"And just what is it that I will be looking for along the way?"

"You're the one that said it, George," said Rider.

"Said what?"

"Maybe he had a stash somewhere out there. See if you can find it."

After George left, Rider went to the front door. He shut the door and slid the bolt into place. The door was solid and the bolt was firm. If Beehunter had told the truth, and Rider still believed that he had, there was no way anyone could have come through that door with the bolt in place. He checked the back door with the same results. Then he went around to each window, carefully examining each in turn. He learned nothing new.

He went outside through the front and shut the door. A little gray dog ran toward him wagging its tail. It stopped a few feet away and ducked its head as if waiting for some sign from the man. Rider squatted and held out his hand.

" '*Siyo,* pup," he said. The dog sneaked on up to within Rider's reach, and Rider scratched it between the ears. Then he stood up to examine the door from the outside.

There was no sign that anyone had even tried to gain entry through that door while it had been locked. Rider then walked around the building, the dog at his heels, checking the windows from the outside, deliberately leaving the window of the death cell for last.

On the west side of the building he noticed a footprint near the wall, near one of the windows in fact. He studied it carefully, but it was not a clear print. It was clearly a footprint, however. As he examined it, the dog sniffed at it as if trying to help.

"Well, dog," said Rider, "somebody was out here."

He noticed nothing else out of the ordinary until he had gone around the building to the east side and was standing just beneath the window of the death cell. There he saw the unmistakable prints of a horse, along with fairly fresh horse droppings, in which the dog showed a special interest. The horse had been standing parallel to the building and close, so close that if a man had been in the saddle, the man's leg would have brushed against the wall.

Rider stepped back and studied the wall. He couldn't be sure, because of the rough sandstone from which the building had been constructed, but he did think that he could see indications of where something had brushed against the wall recently. He believed that it must have been the right leg of the rider.

He hurried back inside and back up to the cell for a closer look at the windowsill. There was a layer of dust on the sill, there were clear marks in the dust: finger marks where someone had grasped the ledge from outside, and what appeared to be the marks made by someone's arms reaching in through the bars.

So it had happened from outside, and the man had stood on the back of a horse in order to see into and reach through the window. That was part of the answer. The angle of the shot was still a puzzle, as were the powder burns on the shirt. And there was the bit of buffalo fur. There was also the strange fact, perhaps the strangest of all, that Beehunter had heard no shot.

But Rider was pleased nevertheless. He was making progress. The deed had been done from outside. He was sure of it now. He might not yet be able to prove it, but he was sure. He went back outside to stand under the window again, and he noticed that the little dog was gone. He tried to follow the tracks of the horse that had stood underneath the window, but they moved across the yard and out onto Water Street. From there they were lost. There had already been heavy traffic along there during the day.

Rider was disgusted with himself. If he had noticed those tracks first thing in the morning, he might have been able to follow them on down the street. This late on a busy day it was impossible.

He went back into his office and poured a cup of coffee, then sat down behind his desk with his feet up to wait for the return of George Tanner and to think.

When George stepped into the office he had a bottle in each hand. Both were empty.

"It's not exactly a stash," he said, "but it is a little unusual."

He placed the bottles on the desk top in front of Rider. Rider sat up straight and looked hard at the labels.

"I ain't seen any of that kind around here before," he said.

"Yeah. That's what I thought. But that's not all."

George had a smug smile on his face and his arms crossed over his chest.

"Well, what, George?" said Rider. "Am I supposed to guess or what?"

George shrugged, reached forward, and picked up one of the bottles by its neck. He waved the bottle under Rider's nose.

"Take a whiff of that," he said.

"Whew."

Rider brushed the bottle aside and wrinkled his face.

"It smells like most other booze I've smelt," he said. "What's the matter with you?"

George put the bottle down and picked up the other one. He held that one out toward Rider.

"Try this one now," he said, and when Rider hesitated, he added, "Go on."

Rider gave George a puzzled look, took the bottle from him, and gave it a tentative sniff. He glanced up at George again, then sniffed a little harder at the bottle.

"I don't smell nothing here, George," he said, "except maybe — wait a minute." He sniffed again. "Sassafras."

"That's what I thought."

"What do you make of it?" Rider asked.

"Well," said George, "ordinarily I probably wouldn't make anything at all of it, but with what all we already know about Eli Martin and the events of last night, I'd say that it might mean that someone met Martin at the sale barn or somewhere between there and here and deliberately got him drunk."

"This other fellow, whoever he was," said Rider, "had two bottles. The one with booze in it he gave to Martin, and he pretended to be drinking along with him, only all the time he was just drinking sassafras tea. Is that it?"

"Well, it's possible. Of course, it's also possible that someone else entirely tossed these two bottles out there."

"This is good, George," said Rider. "Real good. You still got your horse out there?"

"Yeah."

"Come on." Rider led the way back outside. "Mount up," he said, "and follow me."

George climbed into the saddle while Rider

walked around to the west side of the building. He stopped underneath the window there in the middle of the wall. It was almost exactly the same height off the ground as was the window on the east side.

"Ride up right here," he said, "just as close to the wall as you can get."

George did as Rider had said.

"Okay. What now?"

Rider moved up and took hold of the horse's halter to hold him steady.

"Stand up in the saddle, George," he said.

"What?"

"Stand up in the saddle. Go on."

George groaned in feigned protest, then struggled up to stand in the saddle. He turned his head and found himself looking right through the window into the cell.

"Okay," said Rider, "come on down."

When George was standing on the ground beside him, Rider dropped the horse's reins and let them trail on the ground.

"Now," he said, "look here. Look at the marks you made on the wall."

George studied the wall for a moment and nodded his head slowly.

"Okay," he said.

"Follow me," said Rider.

He led George around the building to the east wall, stopping near the cell window, and looked down at the ground toward the footprint and the hoof prints.

"Somebody's been here," said George.

"And look at the wall," said Rider.

"Yeah. Yeah, I see what you mean. It does look like someone climbed up there. I made marks on the other wall similar to these."

Rider then took George back inside and upstairs to the cell to show him the marks in the dust on the windowsill. Then they went back down to the office and sat down. For a moment they were silent. George seemed particularly thoughtful.

"Rider," he said.

"Yeah?"

"It's sure starting to look like you were right. There's still some questions, but it's starting to look that way. I should've known. I guess I owe you an apology."

"You don't owe me nothing, George," said Rider, "but I think you might owe one to Beehunter."

George just stared ahead blankly for a moment.

"Yeah," he said. "I sure do."

Chapter 10

Beehunter was worried. A man had been murdered, and it sure looked like it was his fault. He knew that. He even felt like it was his fault. He had been on duty in the jail when it happened. The building had been locked up tight, and no one had been inside except the prisoner and Beehunter. The man had been shot at close range. No one could have done that from outside. And it seemed as if no one could have gotten inside and back out again.

Beehunter could think of only one way it could have happened. Only one thing made any sense to his Cherokee way of looking at the world. Someone who had it in for either the murdered man or for Beehunter himself had gone to an Indian doctor, a conjurer, and the conjurer, using his mysterious powers, had caused the man's death. There were people with that kind of power who were unscrupulous enough to do that sort of thing. He knew that.

Beehunter had heard all of his life that one

way to kill a *tsgili,* a witch, was to get a doctored bullet from an Indian doctor. Then, it was said, one could simply point the gun in any direction and fire it. The bullet would find the *tsgili.* Perhaps a bullet could be doctored for other purposes as well, not just to protect one from a witch, but to murder someone.

Or perhaps the man in the cell had himself been a *tsgili* that someone was after with a doctored bullet. If that was the case, then Beehunter was simply an innocent victim. He just happened to be there when the bullet found its mark. The person who fired the bullet likely did not even know where it had gone.

Beehunter wondered whether or not Go-Ahead Rider was thinking about these kinds of possibilities. Go-Ahead had not given any indication that he might be thinking in that direction. But what else could he think? That someone had walked through the doors? That Beehunter was lying? That Beehunter was guilty of the murder?

Even if Go-Ahead Rider was only thinking that Beehunter had let him down, that was enough in itself to give Beehunter pain. Go-Ahead trusted him, and Beehunter could hardly stand the thought that he might have somehow betrayed that trust. There was no one in the world that Beehunter liked, admired, and respected as much as he did Go-Ahead Rider.

And there was another thing that was bothering Beehunter. If, in fact, bad medicine had somehow been used to accomplish the killing in the jail, the buffalo fur was almost surely a part of it, and Beehunter had touched the buffalo fur, had held it in his hand for several minutes.

He rode to the home of White Tobacco, a few miles outside of Tahlequah in the woods. When he arrived, he found the old man sitting underneath the brush arbor that stood just beside his house. Beehunter stopped his horse a respectable distance away from the arbor and tied it there. He took off his gun belt and hung it over the saddle horn. Then he walked toward the arbor.

"'*Siyo, Jola Unega,*" he said.

" '*Siyo,* Beehunter. Come in and sit with me here."

White Tobacco had four old straight-backed chairs sitting there under his arbor. Beehunter took one of them and sat down.

"*Tohiju?*" he said.

"I'm doing well," said the old man. "*Nihina?*"

"I have a problem," said Beehunter. "That's why I've come to see you."

"Of course I knew that," said White Tobacco. He was filling his pipe bowl as he spoke. "Tell me about it."

"You know that I sometimes work for Go-Ahead Rider."

"Yes. I know. You're one of the catchers," said White Tobacco, using the Cherokee word for a lawman.

"I was working last night. There was a prisoner in one of the cells. He was drunk and passed out. I was left to spend the night with him, and while I was there, while the building was locked, somebody killed him. It looks like I did it, but I didn't."

"You mean someone killed this man from outside a locked building?" asked White Tobacco. He struck a match and lit his pipe.

"Yes," said Beehunter, "or someone got in through locked doors and back out again. The other thing is, the man was shot from up close, inside the building, and I heard no shot.

"And there was fur from a buffalo on the man, stuck to his shirt there where the bullet went in. I touched it."

White Tobacco sat for a long while in silence, puffing on his pipe. Clouds of protective smoke hovered momentarily around his head, then rose slowly to gather just below the roof of the arbor and slowly seep through between the branches and leaves to rise on up into the sky above to dissipate. He put the pipe down on an empty chair seat and stood up.

"Wait for me here," he said, and he went into his log cabin and shut the door. Beehunter had a pretty good idea of what White Tobacco was up to. He figured that

106

the old man had gone inside to consult a crystal. He knew that was one of the ways in which the Indian doctors read events of the past or of the future. There were other ways, but usually, he thought, when the doctor went into the house, that was what he was doing.

In a few minutes White Tobacco came back out carrying something in each hand. He resumed his seat there under the arbor. He rocked his chair back on the two rear legs and stared at the ground there between himself and Beehunter. Then he reached forward to hand something to Beehunter. Beehunter took it, and then he could tell that it was a chunk of lye soap, homemade and wrapped in paper. Then White Tobacco handed him the packet from the other hand, a bag of tobacco.

"Wash yourself with that soap," he said. "Smoke the tobacco four times a day for protection, and look for the whiskey man."

Go-Ahead Rider struck a match and lit the tobacco in his corncob pipe. Then he leaned his chair back and put his feet up on top of his desk. Puffing at his pipe, he stared at the items lined up there in front of him on the desk: two whiskey bottles, a piece of lead, a shirt with two bullet holes in it — powder burns at the entry hole, and a bit of buffalo fur.

He heard the front door open, and in a moment, Judge Harm Boley walked in.

"Hello, Harm," said Rider. "Two visits in one day. It must be serious."

"I'd say so," said Boley. "Go-Ahead, you've got to put Beehunter under arrest. I know how you feel about him, and I'm sorry, but this murder's being talked about all over town, and now the council's even talking about it. And I mean in session. If you don't do something real soon, I'm afraid that they're going to take some kind of official action."

"Harm, they pay me to do this job. Why don't you just tell them to let me do it? I'd have thought they had enough to worry about with us about to lose six million acres of land."

"Damn it, there was no one here who could have fired that shot except for Beehunter. Now I think you've put it off long enough."

Rider puffed on his pipe and waited. Boley was pacing about the room, but he seemed to have quit talking.

"Are you done?" said Rider.

"I've said what I came to say, if that's what you mean."

"All right, now you listen to me for a minute. I ain't been just sitting here all day. Now I'm going to tell you this one time, and I want you to listen good. Beehunter didn't shoot nobody, and Beehunter didn't tell no lies.

"I know that Eli Martin was killed from outside the jailhouse by somebody just outside the cell window. I don't know all the details yet, but if you and the councilmen will leave me alone so that I can think, I'll get it figured out."

Boley stared hard at Rider, just the way, Rider thought, a white man would stare. But then, Boley was actually more white than Indian. A lot of Cherokee citizens were like that, more and more all the time, it seemed.

"Tell me what you know, Rider," the judge said.

Rider told him everything. He told him about the whiskey bottles and the theory he and George had worked out. Then he told him about the hoofprints and the footprint underneath the window and the marks on the wall and on the windowsill. He told him how he had made George imitate the theorized actions and how, by standing on his horse's back, George had been able to look right in through the cell window, and how in the process of going through those motions, George had made marks on the wall similar to those Rider had observed beneath the window of the death cell.

"I've just got four more questions left to answer, Harm," he said, "and then it'll all be done except for the arrest."

"Well, then, what are they?" asked the judge.

"I can explain how the man got up to the

window and got his arms inside the cell, but I still can't figure out how to explain the angle of the bullet wound."

"That's one."

"I can't tell you why Beehunter never heard the shot."

"Two."

"Three and four are who did the shooting and why?"

"All right, Go-Ahead," said Boley. "I'll do my best to hold them off. You just do your best to get those four questions answered. The sooner the better."

Hoak Fletcher was getting tired. Driving a wagon load of hay from Tahlequah almost to Seneca, Missouri, made for a long day, but Hoak kept telling himself that it should all turn out to be well worth while in the long run. He knew there were plenty of folks around who would pay well for a bottle or two of good whiskey instead of the typical rotgut that was generally available in the Cherokee Nation. And if he could load the stuff up, hide it under the hay and get back to Tahlequah by tomorrow night, he should find plenty of ready customers right there gathered in one spot. That was the beauty of these national council meetings.

The Missouri line was not far ahead, and Hoak was glad of that. His back was aching from leaning over the reins, and his rump was sore from riding all day on the wooden wagon seat. It was dark already, and he didn't like driving alone on the lonely back roads after dark. The country was full of road agents, cutthroats, and thieves of all stripes. An honest businessman just wasn't safe out alone like that. He reached over to the shotgun that rested on the seat beside him. Just feeling it in his grip gave him a sense of some security and comfort.

He figured in another few miles he'd be at Joe Carter's place, and it would be none too soon. He'd give Carter the note he had gotten from Thomson and have Carter put him up for the night. Then in the morning he'd load up the whiskey and head back for Tahlequah in plenty of time to do a little bit of business that very night.

The whiskey would be well hidden under the hay in the back of the wagon. There would be nothing to call attention to him, so he shouldn't have any trouble on the return trip. He would only have to find a good place to work from. That's all. Thomson had told him that he'd be able to double his money, and he believed that was true. That greedy thought stiffened his back a little. It was only a few more miles to Carter's place.

Chapter

11

Early the next morning, just after Rider left home to go to his office, Exie and Tootie and Buster, taking a big picnic basket with them, left the house too. They went down from the bluff to where the tents were lined up along Wolfe Creek, and in a short while they had located the wife and children of Earl Bob. Earl Bob's wife Akie and Exie were cousins, and the children were good friends. By some happy coincidence, Akie's daughter Lula was just about the same age as Tootie, and her son Jali was about Buster's age. The children always got along with each other very well. With Rider gone all day during the council meeting, a day at the creek with Akie and the children would be a pleasant diversion.

Down along the creek, women cooked or visited with each other, one eye on their children who ran up and down the creek, and even in and out of it. Some men, mostly older men, sat around smoking and visiting with one another, but most of the men had gone up into the town.

Buster and Jali chased each other, one occasionally catching the other and throwing him to the ground, laughing all the time. They ran into the space between Earl Bob's campsite and that of their nearest neighbor to the north. It was a nice wide space in which to play. They wrestled there for a few minutes before Jali noticed the pole. It was a nice long cane pole just lying there neglected, abandoned, he assumed.

"Look," he said, talking in Cherokee to Buster, "a fishing pole."

"Whose is it?" said Buster.

"Nobody's. It's just here. Let's take it and go fishing."

"We need some line," said Buster.

"Here's some. Just right here by the pole. Plenty of line. We just need to tie it back up. See. The things are still here on the pole to put the line through. Come on. Help me."

"We'll need a hook," said Buster.

"Well, we'll find one somewhere or else make one. Come on."

"Wait a minute," said Buster. "There's more line here."

"That's just little short pieces," said Jali. "They're no good. Come on."

"Okay. Maybe we'll catch a whole mess of fish and our mamas can cook them for us."

Jali was running ahead of Buster by then, and Buster yelled out after him.

"Hey, can you clean them?" he said.

"Sure I can. Come on."

George Tanner was just finishing his breakfast. Lee poured him another cup of coffee. "Stop worrying about yesterday, George," she said. "Yesterday's gone. Just have a better day today. That's all."

George heaved a heavy sigh.

"I guess you're right," he said, "but I just feel so — well, sort of stupid. No. It's worse than that. I feel almost like a traitor. To Beehunter and to Rider. I'm almost ashamed to face them."

George had told Lee about the murder and how it had looked initially. He had told her that in spite of the way things looked, Rider had never doubted Beehunter, but George had. He had even gone so far as to tell Rider that he was letting his feelings for Beehunter cloud his vision. Then he had told her how Rider had figured out more or less what had happened outside the window.

"It's all behind you now, George," she said. "Didn't you say that even Judge Boley had believed that Beehunter was guilty? It wasn't just you. You weren't alone. So now just go back to work and help Rider figure out the rest of it. And stop worrying about what's past."

"All right," he said. "You're right, of course. As usual."

He stood up to get his hat. It was time for

him to be getting on down to the jail.

"So, now then, let's talk about you," he said. "What will you be doing with yourself all this long day today while I'm out trying to solve a murder?"

"Oh, I don't know. Don't worry about me, though. I'll be all right. I will be glad when school starts up again, though. These summer days alone at home can seem pretty long and dull. The house is so clean it squeaks. It's almost embarrassingly clean, if you can accept that notion."

"Say," said George, "Rider said something yesterday about Exie and the kids going down to the creek. Earl Bob's family is camping out down there. Why don't you go down there and visit with them?"

Lee picked up some dishes from the table and carried them over to the counter. She cocked her head to one side as if in thought.

"Well," she said, "that sounds like a good idea. I could take along some fried chicken or something. Maybe I will do that."

Matt Thomson came out the front door of the National Hotel feeling fresh and cocky. He had money in his pockets and the promise of more, much more, where that had come from. He was free and clear. He had eliminated the one man who could connect him with Albert Palmer in St. Louis, and as far as he could tell, the sheriff and his deputies

115

were totally befuddled over the killing. He decided to take a stroll along Muskogee Avenue past the capitol building.

It was a nice day, pleasant, not too warm, although it looked to Thomson like it might get that way later in the day. As he approached the square, he saw the five deputies standing there together with Go-Ahead Rider. They must be getting their day's instructions from the sheriff, he thought. He walked closer, stopping only when he reached the low rail fence that enclosed the square.

"Good morning, sheriff," he called out.

Rider looked over his shoulder to see who was there. Then, recognizing Thomson, he touched the brim of his hat in response to the greeting. Earl Bob looked that way too, and when he saw Thomson, he smiled and waved.

"Good morning there, neighbor," he said.

Thomson waved casually and then strolled on his way.

"Where do you know that fellow from, Earl Bob?" Rider asked.

"Oh, he camped out beside us night before last," said Earl Bob. "We gave him something to eat. Said he was going to go fishing."

"You said night before last. He didn't stay there, then, last night?"

"No. Just the one night. He packed up and left the next morning. I never seen him again till just now. Something wrong, Rider?"

"No," said Rider. "Nothing." He turned his head back toward where Thomson had been standing just a moment ago and stared for a couple of seconds, seemingly lost in thought. Then he turned back to the deputies.

"Well, boys," he said, "I better be getting back over to the jailhouse. I opened up before I came over here and left everything standing open."

"It's okay, Rider," said Delbert Swim, one of the deputies. "I just seen George go in a minute ago."

Rider glanced toward the jail.

"Oh, good," he said. "Well, I need to get back, anyhow. You boys take up your posts. The councilmen ought to start showing up here any minute now. We need to look alive. Maybe if they think we're doing our job, they'll get on with theirs."

"And leave us alone?" said Earl Bob.

"You said it, Earl Bob. Not me."

Rider walked back toward Water Street instead of cutting across the lawn. He figured that his family might be over there at the creek by that time, and he hadn't seen Earl Bob's family yet to say hello to them. He thought he'd just walk over that way for a couple of minutes. He wasn't really all that anxious to get back inside the office anyway.

They were easy to find. Earl Bob's tent was set up almost directly behind the capitol square down on the creek. Akie had some coffee made, and Rider took a cup. Tootie and Lula were sitting together not far away talking like they had important business which had to be kept secret from everyone else. Buster and Jali were nowhere to be seen.

"They've been running all over the place," said Akie.

"In and out of the creek even," said Exie.

"They found a cane pole somewhere, so now they think they're going to catch some fish," Akie added.

Rider finished his coffee and excused himself to head back toward his office. He had just started to cut through the space where Thomson had camped for the one night, and he stopped. He thought a moment, then turned around to call back toward the Earl Bob camp.

"Akie," he said.

"Yes? What?"

"Is this where Matthew Thomson camped out the other night? This place right here?"

"I don't know the man's name," said Akie, "but there was a man there night before last."

"Earl Bob said you fed him."

"Yes. That one. He was right there."

"Thanks, Akie," said Rider. He stood there in the open space just staring at the ground and thinking. For some reason he was curious about the man Thomson. Maybe it was even more than curiosity. He was suspicious of him. For the killing of Martin? Maybe. He had no real reason to be suspicious of Thomson. Was it just the way the man looked? Something about his behavior, his attitude? The way he had come into the office to announce himself? Why had he done that anyhow? If he was the killer that had been a bold move. Was the man that arrogant, that cocksure? Rider decided that he would sure like to know some more about Matthew Thomson.

He turned slowly, looking over the former campsite. He could see where Thomson's horse had been. He saw no evidence of a fire. But Thomson had eaten with Earl Bob's family, and, it seemed, abandoned the campsite the next day. Rider found a spot where he thought Thomson must have spread his bedroll and slept that night. The grass was mashed down there in just about the right shape. And there beside the spot where he had slept were some short pieces of what looked like fishing line.

What did that mean? Maybe nothing. Probably nothing. Rider picked up the pieces and put them in a pocket. He looked around once more and saw nothing unusual, nothing more of any interest. After all, the man had only slept there one night, and he had not eaten there at all, had not even built a fire. Rider told himself that he could not reasonably expect to find much under those circumstances.

He walked back toward Water Street, but he did not walk straight out toward the street. He cut across at an angle, taking the shortest route toward the jail. He was about to step out into the street when he noticed the gray pup off in the tall grass. It had something between its teeth and was shaking its head as if to kill it. It looked to Rider like some kind of small furry animal. And when the pup stopped shaking its head, the animal did not move. The pup had killed it. Or, what was more likely, had found it already dead.

"What you got there, pup?" Rider said. The pup backed away from Rider a little, stopped, and shook the thing vigorously, growling through its teeth. Rider smiled and walked on toward the jail. Then all of a sudden the dog was trotting along beside him, the thing still clenched in its teeth. Rider looked down at the pup. The thing in its mouth had a strange appearance. He dropped down into a squat and held out his hands.

"Come here, pup," he said. "Come on."

The dog moved up close enough for Rider to pat its head and then to rub its back. Rider looked at the thing in its mouth as he patted the scruffy-looking mutt. It was not a small animal at all. It looked like a mitten. What was more, it looked strangely like the fluff of buffalo hair he had on his desk. He took hold of it with one hand, still patting the dog with the other.

"You going to let me have this?" he said. "Come on now. That's a good pup."

He took the mitten out of the dog's mouth, gave the dog a few more scratches between the ears, and stood up.

"Come on," he said. "Come along."

Strange, he thought, as he walked on toward the office, the dog trotting along beside him, for someone to drop a mitten out here in this kind of weather. And it did not have the appearance of having lain there for a long time. Then he saw the dark stains, and he examined it more closely. There was a hole in the end of the mitten, in the middle of the dark stains. Bloodstains, Rider thought. And powder burns. And is that for sure buffalo hide? he asked himself. And he answered, I think it is.

Rider hurried back to the office. The dog followed him inside. George was sitting at the small desk with a cup of coffee. He looked up when he heard Rider come in, and he looked down distastefully at the dog.

"Good morning, Rider," he said. "What's that?"

Rider moved quickly over to his own desk.

"Never mind, George," he said, "look at this. Look here."

George moved over to stand beside Rider, and Rider tossed the mitten down on the desk beside the piece of fur he had taken from the shirt of the murdered man. George looked but said nothing. Rider picked up the mitten and shoved his right hand into it, poking a finger out through the hole in the end.

"Rider," said George, "is that what I think it is?"

"It looks like it to me, George. That look like bloodstains there around the hole?"

"It sure does."

"And powder burns?"

"Yes, sir. I think so."

Rider picked up the bit of buffalo fur from the desk top and held it beside the mitten.

"And that's the same stuff," said George. "Rider, the gun that killed Martin was inside that mitten, and it was held against Martin's chest when it was fired."

"That's right."

"Where did you find it?"

Rider gestured with a jut of his chin toward the dog, which sat just at his left leg, wagging its tail and panting.

"He brought it to me," he said. "I never found it at all. Not by my own self."

"Rider, do you think that could have muffled the sound of the shot? You know, enough to explain why Beehunter didn't hear it?"

"I can't think of any other reason for it to have been done this way, George," said Rider.

"But let's find out for sure. Only first, I want you to run over and get Judge Boley. Bring him over here. I want him to see this, and I want him to witness our little experiment."

"Yes, sir. I'll be right back with him, Rider," said George. "Oh, yeah. There's something else. I don't know what it means."

"What's that?"

"Take a look at the whiskey bottles there on your desk. I noticed that when I came in this morning. 'Course you'd already been here. Maybe you already saw it."

Rider turned back to his desk. The two bottles still stood there side by side, as he had left them the night before, but the label was torn off one of the bottles. Just one. Rider put a hand to his chin and stared at the bottle.

"I'd swear it wasn't like that when I came in this morning, George," he said. "Now who'd a done that? And why?"

"It beats me," said George.

"Well, go on and get the judge over here," said Rider.

George hurried on out the door, and Rider moved around behind his desk. He sat down, put his feet up, and stared at the accumulation of evidence there before him. The gray dog had followed. It stretched itself out on the floor just to the right of Rider's chair.

Chapter 12

Beehunter rode up to a lonely cabin in the woods. As he was swinging down out of his saddle, the front door of the cabin was pushed open from the inside, and a dark face peered out through the opening.

"'*Siyo*," said Beehunter. "I came to buy some whiskey."

"Come in," said the man.

Beehunter went inside the cabin. It was messy. A woman sat on the edge of a rumpled bed. Beehunter nodded to her, but she didn't acknowledge his greeting. The man went around behind the bed and bent over to reach under it. He straightened up with a groan and produced a jug.

"No," said Beehunter. "I want this kind."

He pulled the label from the whiskey bottle on Rider's desk out of his pocket and held it out for the man to see.

"I don't have that," said the man. "This kind is good enough to get drunk on."

"No," said Beehunter. "This is what I want. Where can I find it?"

"Nobody around here has that kind," said the man. "You'll have to take this if you want whiskey."

"No," said Beehunter, and he left the cabin. He made two more similar stops. At the second place, the scene played out was almost identical to the first one. At the third, the man in the house denied having any whiskey at all to sell.

Beehunter thought hard. Even though he was not a full-time deputy, the fact that he worked sometimes as a special deputy for Go-Ahead Rider made many of the dealers in illegal spirits afraid to confide in him. Still, he knew who many of them were. But after the first three tries he couldn't think of anyone else except some who might be operating out of wagons and secret temporary locations around Tahlequah, so he turned his horse toward the capital city.

George opened the front door and stepped aside to allow Judge Harm Boley to enter first. Boley went on inside and into the office, and as George was walking in behind him, Boley said, "Well, where is he?"

George looked around the office. There was no sign of Rider, nor, George noted with satisfaction, of the dog.

"Well, Judge," he said, "I don't know. He told me to run over to your office and bring you right back here. That's all I know."

He stepped out into the hallway and was about to call out Rider's name in case he had gone upstairs for some reason, but just as he opened his mouth, the front door opened, and Rider stepped in.

"Oh," said George. "We were just wondering where you were."

Rider held out an open palm to reveal a small pocket pistol.

"I thought we ought to do this right," he said. "Is Harm in there?"

"Yes, sir."

"Come on."

They went into the office where Boley was pacing the floor.

"Rider," said the judge, "what's this all about?"

"Remember my four questions?" Rider asked.

"Yes."

"I got an answer to one of them. Look over here."

Rider led the judge to the edge of his desk. He picked up the lead.

"I found this on the floor of the cell," he said. "I believe that it's the bullet that killed Martin, and it appears to be about a forty-one caliber."

"So?" said Boley.

"Just hold your horses, Judge," said Rider, and he picked up the bit of buffalo fur. "You remember this?"

"Yes, I do."

126

"All right then. Now look at this."

Rider handed the mitten to Judge Boley, who took it and studied it with genuine interest. Then he handed it back to Rider.

"Go on," he said.

"Well, I ran out just now to borrow this little forty-one-caliber pocket pistol. I figure that something kind of like this was used. The caliber's right, and the whole thing will go up inside this mitten here. You can see on this mitten here on the end where a bullet was fired through it. There's bloodstains, and there's powder burns. Did you notice that?"

"Yes, I did," said Boley, sounding a little impatient, "and I think I know where you're going with this, so let's just get on with it."

Rider handed the pistol to George, then handed him the mitten.

"That thing's loaded, George," he said. "Shove her up in there. Go up to the cell and fire it off."

"Yes, sir," said George. He took the pistol and the mitten and hurried out of the office. Rider went back behind his desk and sat down. Boley still paced in front of the desk. Then they heard a muffled sound, not very loud.

"That was it?" asked Boley.

Rider waited, and in a moment George came back into the office.

"Well?" he said. "Did you hear it?"

"I take back what I said about arresting Beehunter," said the judge. "He's in the

127

clear. Someone shot Martin from outside, and he muffled the shot with that mitten. All right. Find out who did it."

Boley left the office, and George looked at Rider and smiled.

"We still got a problem, George," said Rider.

"How did the killer reach through the bars far enough to press the gun right up against Martin's chest."

"Yeah. Let's try that."

"Okay," said George. "How?"

"You go down to the barn and saddle up a horse and bring him around under the window again. I'm going up to the cell."

"You're going to be Martin, and I'm going to be the killer. Right?"

"Right."

When George once again stood in the saddle outside the cell, Rider stood on the cell floor looking out. George reached an arm through the cell and poked a finger against Rider's chest just about where Martin had been shot.

"But angled like this," said Rider, turning George's hand so that the imaginary bullet would go in the left side of the chest but come out the right side of the back.

"Why would I twist my hand like that?" said George.

"You wouldn't," said Rider. "The other

128

thing is, if you were to shoot me now, I'd fall straight back on the floor. I sure wouldn't be able to get myself over there on the cot to wind up laid out real nice the way Martin was."

"No," said George. "I don't see how you could. Hey. Whoa there." The horse beneath him had taken a step forward to reach what it believed to be better looking grass. "Rider," George said, "can I get down now?"

"In a minute," said Rider. He moved over to the cot and stretched out on it. "Now, George," he said, "see how close you can get?"

George reached through the bars as far as he could with his right arm, stretching it out to the right, toward Rider there on the cot.

"No way, Rider," he said. "Forget it."

"Okay, George," said Rider. "You can get down now."

Beehunter was on Muskogee Avenue at the north end of town. It was not quite as crowded there as farther south toward the capitol, but there were still quite a few people walking up and down, and the horse and wagon traffic out in the street was heavy. Beehunter lounged against a storefront watching the faces of the men who passed. Then he stopped one.

"*'Siyo,*" said the man. "I haven't seen you for a while, Beehunter." The man spoke in

Cherokee. Beehunter answered him in a low voice.

"I want some whiskey," he said. "You have any to sell?"

"No. I don't have any whiskey."

"I know you," said Beehunter. "You always have whiskey. That's what everybody says about you. You always have whiskey to sell. Sell me some."

"If I had any whiskey, I wouldn't sell it to you. You work for Go-Ahead Rider. You're a catcher. You think I'm stupid?"

"I'm not working anymore," said Beehunter. "They think I killed that man in the jail. I need some whiskey."

"Well, I don't know."

"Come on," said Beehunter. "Wait a minute. Look at this." He reached into his pocket and pulled out the label. "You have this kind?"

"No," said the man. "I don't have any of that."

"Where can I get this kind?"

"I don't know. If anyone has that I bet it's a white man. I don't have that."

Beehunter put the label back in his pocket and leaned back against the wall again. "Okay," he said, and he resumed researching the faces of the passersby.

It was about noon, and Go-Ahead Rider was walking along Muskogee Avenue. He was looking for Matthew Thomson. He had already gone to the National Hotel to inquire, so he knew that Thomson was still in town. He had not checked out of his room. Rider stopped at every diner to look inside. Thomson was likely getting himself some lunch someplace. At the fourth place he looked, he found his man.

He went inside and over to the table where Thomson sat alone eating a steak. He pulled out a chair and sat down.

"Do you mind?" he said.

"No. Of course not, Sheriff. I'm glad for the company. You want something to eat?"

"Just a cup of coffee," said Rider.

Thomson flagged down the waiter and ordered the coffee.

"How's your investigation going?" he asked.

"Not bad," said Rider. "We've proved that Beehunter didn't do it."

"Beehunter?"

"Oh, that's the name of my deputy, the one who was in the building that night."

"You say —" The waiter came with the coffee, and Thomson stopped talking. The man put down a cup for Rider, then filled it and refilled Thomson's cup. When he had done, Thomson resumed his talk. "You say you've proved he didn't do it? How could you do that?"

"Someone shot Martin from outside," Rider said. "He rode a horse up close to the wall and stood up on his saddle. That's how he got to the window from outside."

"But your deputy said that he didn't hear a shot. Isn't that right?"

"The shot was fired from a forty-one-caliber pocket pistol that was stuck into a heavy buffalo-hide mitten to muffle the sound. I found the mitten, and we tried it out. It works."

For the first time, Thomson felt serious panic well up from deep inside him. He tried to keep it from showing, and he hoped that his effort was working, but he couldn't be sure. Damn, he thought. The son of a bitch is on to me. He's figured it out.

"A mitten?" he said. "Well, I'd never have thought of that. A mitten to muffle the sound. I'll be damned. Somebody must have put a lot of thought into that one."

He suspects me, he said to himself, but he hasn't got any proof. If he had any proof, he'd arrest me. Damn. He found the mitten. Where the hell could he have found it? I retraced all my steps, and I didn't find it. He took a swallow of his coffee.

"Well, uh, so it was done from outside. Do you know who did it then?" he asked.

Rider turned up his own coffee cup and drained it. He put the cup back down on the table.

"Well, I haven't got all the proof yet," he said, "but I've got a pretty good idea. It won't be long now. See you around, Mr. Thomson."

He stood up, walked to the counter and paid for his coffee, then left the diner. Thomson stared after him. His whole world had just been turned upside down. He had felt so sure of himself, so proud even, and now, he thought, now this bastard is after me. He knows.

But he said he didn't have all the proof he needed yet. What other proof could there be? The mitten. The other mitten of the pair was at his house. Why hadn't he thought of that? Why hadn't he thrown the other one away? And the gun. Rider had even figured out what kind of gun he had used. He still had the gun in his valise. He would have to get rid of the gun. What else? What else was there?

The cane pole. He had left the cane pole and the line there at the campsite. But it was just a cane pole, a fishing pole in fact. Lots of people had cane poles just like it. What could it prove? And Rider hadn't said anything about a pole. He probably had not figured that part out. Still, he couldn't really take a chance. The sheriff had figured everything else out. He would likely figure out the pole, too, sooner or later.

Should he go back to the campsite and find the pole and get rid of it? One of Rider's deputies was camped there just beside it, and he had seen the pole. Thomson remembered explaining the pole to the man by saying that he was planning to do some fishing. He hadn't known that the man was a deputy until later.

Thomson didn't feel like finishing his meal. He paid for it and left. Walking back toward the hotel, his mind kept spinning. What was best to do? Go-Ahead Rider was on his trail. That much was certain. Then it came to him. There was just one thing to do, one way to be safe. He would have to kill Go-Ahead Rider.

Chapter 13

After he left Thomson, Go-Ahead Rider walked down to the creek to join his family and Earl Bob's family for lunch. Earl Bob was still on duty at the capitol square, and George was at the jail. When Rider arrived at the tent by the creek, he found Lee Tanner there with the others. Everyone was there except the boys.

"They'll show up when they get hungry enough," Exie said.

The women served Rider a plate full of food and a cup of hot coffee. Rider ate his fill and got up to leave.

"I'll send George and Earl Bob on down in just a few minutes," he said. "That was real good, ladies."

Just then the boys came running up.

"Daddy. Daddy," Buster called out in Cherokee. "Jali and I have been fishing."

"Hello, Buster," Rider said, catching the boy up in his arms for just a moment. "Talk English now. Mrs. Tanner's here."

"Oh. Okay. Me and Jali's been fishing."

"Did you catch anything?"

"Not yet," said Jali. "But we're going back after we eat."

"That looks like a pretty good pole you've got there," said Rider. "Can I see it for a minute?"

Jali handed the pole to Rider. The pole had a full set of eyelets, but the line was strung through only the two closest to the small end.

"Well, you don't have enough line on here," said Rider, "and you need a real hook. A cork would be good too."

"We know," said Jali, "but we don't have those things, so we're just using what we got."

Rider looked at the pole, and he thought about the bits of string he had found at the next campsite.

"Where'd you boys get this pole?" he asked.

"Right over there," said Buster, pointing to the former campsite of Matthew Thomson.

"Earl Bob said that Thomson told him he was planning on doing some fishing," Rider said, talking more to himself than to anyone else. Then he spoke up louder again to the boys. "Show me just where you found it, okay?"

The boys ran over to the spot where they had discovered the pole, and Rider followed.

"Right there," said Jali. "The man was

gone. He just left it there."

The boys had pointed out a spot just beside where Rider had already identified the location of Thomson's bedroll. It was also where he had previously picked up the short pieces of fishing line.

"Right here?" Rider said. "Are you sure?"

"Yeah. It was right there," said Jali, leaning over and poking the ground with his finger.

"Boys," said Rider, "I'm going to have to take this pole."

"But we were going to go fishing again," Buster protested.

"You know where my good poles are at, don't you?" Rider said to his son.

"Yeah."

"Well, just as soon as you've had your lunch, you run up to the house and get one for each of you. Okay?"

"One for both of us?" said Jali.

"That's right," said Rider. "Eat your lunch. Then tell your mama that I said you can use them."

"All right," said Buster. "Come on, Jali. Let's go eat."

The boys ran back around to the front of the tent, and Rider could hear their excited voices telling their mothers the good news. He squatted there where the bedroll had been and studied the pole and line. The end of the line the boys had been dangling in the water had a small loop of rawhide tied to it.

Rider untied the line from the pole and strung it back through all the eyelets. The line was almost the same length as the pole. The loop of rawhide was even with the small end. There was a length of line at the opposite end, just enough to get a good hold on and pull. Rider studied the pole and line for a moment.

He reached into his pocket and pulled out the short pieces of line he had picked up earlier there, and he looked at them for a moment. Just then Exie appeared in the small clearing.

"Rider," she said, "something wrong?"

"Huh? Oh, no. No. I'm just thinking. I told Buster to go up to the house and get my poles, one for him and one for Jali. Okay?"

"Okay."

"I'll see you later. I have to get back to work now. Tell the other two ladies their husbands will be along soon. Oh. Send Buster back over here for just a minute, will you?"

"Sure, Rider," said Exie. She went back around to the front of the tent, and a moment later Buster came running back followed by Jali.

"You want me?" he said.

"Buster," said Rider, "was this line already on the pole when you found it?"

"Yeah."

"Did you cut the line?"

"No. It was just that short already."

"There was some other short pieces," said

138

Jali, "but we left them. They were too short."

"And this little piece of leather here," said Rider. "Did you tie this on here?"

"No. It was on there already."

Back in his office, Rider put the pole on his desk top. He took the short pieces of line out of his pocket and put them there beside the pole. Then he moved around behind the desk and sat down.

"What you got there, Rider?" said George.

"I ain't sure yet, George. Lee's down there at Earl Bob's camp. Why don't you run on down there and get yourself something to eat. I'll be here till you get back."

George hesitated a moment, gave a shrug, and said, "Okay." Then he left the office. Rider took the short pieces of line and wrapped them loosely around the small end of the pole. It looked like they could have been tied on there before. They could have been used to tie something on there. Then to take the something off of the end of the pole later, the line had been cut.

He opened a desk drawer and took out the borrowed pocket pistol, then placed it alongside the small end of the pole, wrapping some of the short line around its barrel. Next he slipped the loop of rawhide over the trigger. He stood up and stepped back to admire his handiwork.

"That's it," he said out loud. "That's how he did it."

When George arrived back at the office, he found Rider sitting with his feet on the desk puffing his corncob pipe. He looked somehow pleased with himself, relaxed, almost content.

"You have a good lunch, George?" he said.

"Yeah. Real good. What's that?"

"What?"

"That cane pole on top of your desk."

George walked over to take a closer look. The pocket pistol was still lined up at the end of the pole, the loose line wrapped around pole and gun barrel, the rawhide loop around the trigger.

"That's the rest of our evidence, George," said Rider. "That's what it is."

"Oh, come on, Rider. You mean to tell me that Martin was killed with a rig like that?"

"No," said Rider. "I mean that Eli Martin was killed with that exact rig, all except the pistol."

"That's crazy. I've never seen anything like that in my life."

"Me neither, George. If I had I'd have figured it out a whole lot sooner. You already know that Thomson stood on his horse's back in order to reach the window."

"Hold on a minute," said George. "Hold on. Thomson?"

"Oh yeah. You didn't know that, did you? Matthew Thomson is our killer. Anyhow, you knew how he stood on his horse. Right?"

"Right."

"You knew about the mitten."

"Yeah, but —"

"But when we tried it out, you couldn't reach me inside the cell."

"No way. But —"

"When Thomson first got into town he camped out just beside where Earl Bob's set up down there. He brought a cane fishing pole with him. This one. Earl Bob noticed it and said something about it. Thomson said he was going to try to get in a little fishing.

"Later that night, he took these two bottles here down to the sale barn where he found Eli Martin. He gave Martin the one filled with whiskey, and he drank out of the other one. Probably sassafras tea. Of course, Martin thought they were getting drunk together. They walked on back to town, drinking as they went, and when the bottles were empty, they tossed them off to the side of the road.

"This here is just a guess, but I wouldn't be a bit surprised to find out that it wasn't Martin who hit you with the rock at all."

"Thomson?" said George.

"It was dark out there, and Martin was awful drunk for a good shot like that."

"That's right," said George. "This Thomson could have been behind a tree or something. When I turned around after the rock hit me, I saw Martin staggering along there. I didn't see anyone else, so I assumed that he had thrown the rock."

"You arrested him and put him in a cell, which was just what Thomson had wanted."

"That's a pretty elaborate scheme," said George. "If you're right."

"That's just why it had us fooled for so long," said Rider. "Still later, Thomson tied up this rig, rode his horse over here and killed Martin in a way that made it look like the shooting had been done from inside. It might have worked, too, except for one thing."

"What's that?" asked George.

"I know Beehunter too well. I'd never doubt his word. And then there was that bit of buffalo fur stuck around the wound. It had to get there somehow."

"Okay," said George. "Assuming you're right about how it was done, about this rig here, how do you know this guy Thomson did it?"

"This is his pole, George. He left it at the campsite when he pulled out. Buster and Jali found it and were playing with it today. I found this here over there myself."

He indicated the short pieces of line that had been used to tie the gun to the pole.

"And this rawhide loop here was tied to the line just like it is now when the boys found the pole."

"What about the mitten?" said George.

"Well, he must have dropped that some-where between here and where he was camped. I figure he was carrying the rig back with him, and it dropped off. He didn't notice it, and he didn't think about it when he took the rig apart. Or if he did, maybe he didn't think it was important enough to bother with, or maybe he went back and looked for it in the dark and couldn't find it. Anyhow, old pup found it later. It's animal fur, and it had blood on it. Old pup just naturally sniffed it out."

George sighed and stroked his chin. He paced over to his desk and back again. Then he put his hands on Rider's desk and leaned over the pole and pistol rig as if studying it.

"Just one thing, Rider," he said. "Well, no, two things."

"Yeah?"

"Cane fishing poles are pretty common around these parts. Anyone could have discarded this rig at Thomson's campsite."

"You're right, George. It probably wouldn't convict him in court. The next thing we have to do is find out if Thomson's still packing a fishing pole around with him. If he ain't still got it, then I'd say that pretty well cinches the case against him. You said two things."

"We going to try this rig out to see if it really works?"

"I've been sitting here waiting for you so we could do just that."

"All right," said George. "I'll go get the horse."

Rider stood up with a grin.

"No, George. I'll do that part this time. You fix up something on the cot upstairs for me to shoot into. While you're doing that, I'll tie this gun onto here, and then I'll go get my horse out of the barn."

The gray dog running along beside him, Rider rode up to the side of the jail and dismounted. George handed him the pole. The gun had been loaded and tied securely to the small end of the pole. Rider cocked the pistol, then slipped the rawhide loop carefully over the trigger. He pulled it tight enough to keep it from sliding off. Then he slipped the mitten over the whole thing and climbed up to stand in the saddle.

The dog barked, and the horse fidgeted nervously.

"Whoa, there," said Rider. "George, see if you can keep that pup still."

George knelt down and put a hand on the dog's head, and Rider's horse settled down again. Rider waited a moment until he was relatively certain the horse would keep still. Then he worked the pole in through the bars, and with both his arms stuck through, he moved the pole around and down and pressed the muzzle of the pistol, through the mitten, against the padding that George had prepared on the cot. He held the pole firmly in his right hand, and with his left he pulled on the line. The gun fired.

Rider worked the pole back out through the bars and handed it down to George. Then he got himself down, and led his horse around to the front of the building, where he tied it.

"Come on," he said to George. They went upstairs into the cell, the dog following. Where the bullet had entered the padding there were powder stains and a bit of fur from the mitten. Rider got down on one knee and looked under the cot. He found an exit hole just about where the other one had been. On the floor he found the lead he had fired.

"Rider," said George, "that's it. You were right. I just don't know how you do it."

"Just age and experience, George," said Rider. "I sure ain't smart."

They went over to the capitol building and inside to the office of Judge Harm Boley. Rider told Boley the whole story and asked for a warrant for the arrest of Matthew Thomson. Boley wrote it out immediately and signed it. Armed with the warrant, Rider and George headed for the National Hotel.

"I don't think he's the type to risk resisting arrest, George," Rider said, "but you never know. Stay sharp."

In the lobby of the National, Rider asked for the room number of Thomson.

"He ain't here no more, Rider," said the

clerk. "He checked out earlier today."

"Thanks," said Rider. "Come on, George. Let's go check the stables."

"Say," said George to the clerk. "When Thomson checked in, was he carrying a cane pole, a fishing pole?"

"No."

"Are you sure?"

"I checked him in," said the clerk, "and I remember. All he had was one little bag."

Chapter
14

Rider sent George on back to the jail while he stopped back by the judge's office to tell him that Thomson had slipped through their grasp.

"I'll look around here for him some," he said, "but I expect that he's figured out I'm on to him. I'd like to go up into Delaware District. That's where he lives. I'd like to have a search warrant for his house and property, too."

"Well," said Boley, "I can give you that all right, but you know, if you go up into Delaware District, you'll have to work with Captain Fish."

"Sure," said Rider, "I know that. I'll need his help, anyhow. I don't have no idea where Thomson lives."

"I'll write out a letter, too, to Fish directing him to work with you on this," said Boley. "When do you want to leave?"

"I'd like to head out first thing in the morning," said Rider.

"With the council still in session here?"

"If you'll just authorize me to hire on a

couple more temporary men, I'll leave George in charge here while I'm gone. Everything'll be all right."

"You're not thinking of going up there alone are you?" said Boley. "After a killer?"

"I'll have old Captain Fish along with me, won't I?"

"Well, yeah. I guess you will at that. All right, Rider, you can hire on your two extra men. I might have known you'd figure out a way to get that done. Stop by here on your way out of town. I'll have all the paperwork ready for you."

"Thanks, Harm," said Rider. "See you in the morning."

As Rider left the capitol, the gray dog came running from around the corner and fell into step with him.

" 'Siyo, pup," said Rider. "Where have you been hiding out?"

The sun was low in the sky. It would be dark soon, and Beehunter was still looking for the special whiskey. He had not found any, had not found even any evidence of its presence anywhere near Tahlequah. He was not frustrated nor disappointed, however. He did not think that he had wasted his day. He had discovered where the special whiskey was not available. He was working by the process of elimination. Eventually, he was confident, he would find the source. Beehunter was a very patient man.

And, in addition to his patience and persistence, he had the protection and advice of White Tobacco to bolster his confidence. He also had, he knew, the solid backing of Go-Ahead Rider. It was just a matter of time, he thought.

Now the end of the day was approaching. There were certain places that Beehunter knew about, after-dark hangouts that were known to be reasonably safe havens for both the booze mongers and the consumers of the illegal commodity. He would make the rounds of those places.

Beehunter put his badge and his pistol in his saddlebags and rode to Dogtown, that slightly disreputable settlement just north of Tahlequah. He rode slow and easy through Dogtown, and he saw a couple of clusters of what were almost surely drinkers. But he rode on past them. He was headed for the home of Big Dollar.

Big Dollar and Beehunter were cousins. They had played together as children, and Beehunter had a particular fondness for Big Dollar. But as they grew up, Big Dollar had developed not just a taste but a real need for alcohol, and he wasn't particular about the form it came in. He did, however, seem to know just about every place around, however recent, however temporary, where there was booze to be bought.

Beehunter found Big Dollar at home, sitting

in a chair out in front of the house, drinking.

" 'Siyo, Cousin," he said.

"Beehunter," said Big Dollar, "are you working?"

"No. I just came to see you."

"Come and sit down then. You want a drink?"

Beehunter climbed down off his horse and walked over to sit beside Big Dollar in a chair that didn't seem really very safe.

"What do you have?" he said.

Big Dollar handed a jug to Beehunter. Beehunter took a sniff and handed it back.

"I don't like that kind," he said, "but I'd like to find some of this kind."

He pulled the label out of his pocket and handed it to his cousin. Big Dollar squinted at it in the dim light.

"That costs too much," he said.

"Where did you see it?"

"There's a man with a wagon. He just got here right before dark. I looked at it, but he wanted too much money, so I left. I got this one instead."

"Can you tell me how to find this man?" Beehunter asked.

Big Dollar waved his arm vaguely north.

"He's just out that way. You can find him."

"Why don't you show me? I'll buy you a bottle of this stuff. It's really good, I think."

"You'll buy me a bottle?" said Big Dollar.

"Sure," said Beehunter.

"Not a bottle for us, but a bottle for me?"

"Yes. A bottle of that good stuff for you. If you show me where to get it."

"Let's go," said Big Dollar.

They walked, Beehunter leading his horse. And it wasn't far. They walked north from Big Dollar's house on a rocky road to a left turn down an even more narrow and rocky one. Soon after that they turned right on a narrow lane thickly lined with trees on both sides. Under the trees it was dark, but in a moment they could see light from a small fire. They kept going, and in another minute or so they could see the wagon parked in a clearing. The fire burned on the ground just beside the wagon.

Two men came walking toward Beehunter and Big Dollar from the wagon. As they passed on the lane, they nodded and grunted low and unintelligible greetings. The two men were obviously hiding bottles under their jackets. A few other men were gathered around the wagon. One man made a purchase and turned to leave. By then Beehunter and Big Dollar were there. Two more men paid their money and left.

Standing beside the wagon, Hoak Fletcher looked over the shoulder of the remaining customer ahead of Beehunter and Big Dollar. He spoke to Big Dollar.

"So you come back, eh?" he said. "You can't get nothing else this good around

151

here. That's for sure."

He handed a bottle to the man, who paid him and turned to leave, nodding at Beehunter as he passed him by. Hoak was speaking in English, and so Beehunter did not understand what was being said.

"It costs a little more, sure," Hoak went on, "but it's worth it. It's a better product. Your friend bring some money?"

"He wants your money," Big Dollar said in Cherokee to Beehunter.

Beehunter reached into his pocket and pulled out some cash, which he handed to Big Dollar.

"Get two bottles," he said. "Is that enough money?"

Big Dollar counted the cash in his hand and nodded.

"Two bottles," he said to Hoak, and he handed him the money. Hoak made a little change, which Big Dollar gave to Beehunter. Then Hoak handed two bottles to Big Dollar. Big Dollar handed one of them to Beehunter.

"Thanks," he said to Hoak, then, in Cherokee, to Beehunter, "Let's go."

As they walked away from the wagon, going back down the narrow lane, Hoak called out to them, "Tell your friends. I'll be here all night."

Back at Big Dollar's house, Big Dollar sat back down in his chair and started to open his bottle. Beehunter swung up into his saddle.

"You want to sit here and drink with me?" said Big Dollar.

"No. Thank you, Cousin. I have to go now."

"I wish you'd let me go with you in the morning, Rider," George was saying.

"I'll have all the help I need with Captain Fish," said Rider. "Besides, we don't even know if Thomson'll be at home. I need you to stay here and hold things together, and I need you to be here in case Thomson shows up around here while I'm gone. On top of that, you picked up three drunks while I was out. Things are starting to get a little rowdy around here. I need you here, George. So have you got everything straight?"

"Yes, sir," said George. "Don't worry about anything here."

"I won't as long as you're here," said Rider. "That's the idea. Now I'm about ready to go home and hit the hay. You got everything lined up for tonight?"

"Yeah. Delbert's going to stay here with the prisoners. You go on home and get some sleep."

Rider put on his hat and left the office. George straightened up a few things on his desk. Then he took the coffeepot to the front door and threw out what was left of the coffee. When the liquid splashed on the ground, the gray dog was startled up from where he had been lying against the wall.

"Stupid mutt," said George. He went back inside to wait for Delbert Swim. In a few minutes, he heard a horse approaching outside. In another minute Beehunter came in. He had his saddlebags hanging over his left forearm. He looked a little disappointed. George knew that it was because Rider was gone.

"Beehunter," he said, "what are you doing here?" He felt stupid as soon as he had said it, for, of course, Beehunter had not understood a word he had said.

Beehunter stepped over to George's desk and put his saddlebags down. He opened up one side flap, reached in, and pulled out a bottle of whiskey, which he set down on George's desk top with a loud thump. George recognized the label on the bottle immediately, and he felt his own jaw drop to reveal his astonishment.

"Where'd you get that?" he said, and again he felt stupid.

Beehunter reached into the saddlebag again. This time he brought out his badge and his gun. He pinned the badge on his shirt and tucked the revolver into the waistband of his trousers. Then he motioned to George to follow him.

"*Jinena,*" he said.

"Let's go," was one of the few Cherokee phrases that George understood. He followed

Beehunter outside and looked around almost frantically for any sign of Swim.

"*Jinena*," said Beehunter.

"Wait a minute, will you?" said George. He was about to panic when he saw Swim coming from across the way.

"Delbert," he yelled. "Take over. I've got to go."

He gestured toward the barn back behind the jail. Beehunter mounted his horse and followed George to the barn, where George selected and saddled a horse.

"Okay," he said, and Beehunter kicked his own mount and turned it north. George stayed right behind him. They rode through Tahlequah on Muskogee Avenue, and then they rode the short distance over to Dogtown. From there, Beehunter led the way his cousin had showed him just a short while before. When he reached the turnoff to the narrow lane where the wagon had been parked, Beehunter stopped. He pointed down the lane. George nodded to indicate understanding.

They moved together, side by side down the lane. The small fire still burned. They got closer, and they could see that Hoak was collecting money from a customer. The man took his bottle and turned to walk down the lane. When he saw the two horses coming, he moved off the lane and walked through the tall grass. George and Beehunter let him go. They were after Hoak, though they did not know his name.

Hoak strained to see in the dark who was coming Then he recognized Beehunter.

"Well, hello again, friend," he said. "I didn't expect to see you back so soon. I see you brought me another customer. Good. Come right on up and —"

Just then Hoak noticed the badges. He turned fast, reaching down underneath the wagon seat. Beehunter pulled his revolver out and fired it straight up into the air. Hoak flinched and then stopped moving. George had his own Starr revolver out by then.

"Don't turn around," he said.

"Don't shoot," said Hoak.

"Raise your hands up high."

"All right. All right. Don't shoot."

Hoak, his back still to the deputies, raised his hands.

"Now back away from that wagon," said George. Hoak took a couple of backward steps, and Beehunter slipped down off of his horse's back. He went to the wagon and reached under the seat, pulling out a double-barreled shotgun, which he held up for George to see. Then he walked around to the far side of the wagon. He put the shotgun down in the wagon bed and picked up a bottle by the neck. He held that up for George to see. George nodded in approval.

Then Beehunter climbed up onto the

wagon seat and picked up the reins. George nodded again. Then he spoke to the prisoner.

"Get up on that horse," he said, making a gesture toward Beehunter's mount. "Oh, yeah. By the way, you're under arrest for the introduction of intoxicating liquors into the Cherokee Nation. Mount up."

Hoak climbed into the saddle, and George rode over close to him.

"Put your hands behind your back," he said.

"Wait a minute," said Hoak. "Wait. Can't we work something out here? That wagon load's worth a whole lot of money."

"Be careful," said George. "I'm going to forget you said that, but try it again, and I'll charge you with attempting to bribe an officer of the law. That's almost as serious as selling whiskey. Put your hands behind your back."

Hoak looked at Beehunter and back at George. He put his hands behind him, and George took a pair of handcuffs out of his back pocket. He holstered his Starr and snapped the cuffs onto Hoak's wrists. Then he eased his own horse forward enough to take the reins of the other and lead it along behind him.

"*Jinena*," he said.

Chapter
15

Beehunter and George locked Hoak Fletcher in one cell and, with Delbert Swim's help, unloaded his whiskey into another, then locked it. They took Hoak's wagon and team to the sheriff's barn, unhitched the team and put the horses into stalls. Then they went back to the jail. George unlocked the cell and took Hoak into the office.

"Sit down there," he said, placing a chair in front of his own desk. He went around and sat behind the desk and prepared himself to take notes. Beehunter was sitting in a chair against the opposite wall, silently watching. Swim stood leaning against the door frame.

"What's your name?" said George.

"Horace Fletcher. They call me Hoak."

"Where'd you get that whiskey, Hoak?"

"What whiskey? I don't know what you're talking about. You lawmen are always planting whiskey on folks just so you can get an arrest. I've heard all about that."

"Is that going to be your story?" said

George. "You've got two sheriff's deputies as witnesses against you."

"Two crooked lawmen," said Hoak. "I never seen that stuff until you brought me in here."

"You see those two bottles over there, Hoak?" said George, pointing to the bottles on Rider's desk. Hoak looked at them but said nothing. "You're the only one around here with that brand. I have to think those were your bottles." Still Hoak was quiet. "We think that those two bottles had something to do with the murder that took place right here in this jail a couple of nights ago."

"Wait a minute," said Hoak. "I don't know nothing about that. I heard about it, but I don't know nothing about it. I didn't have nothing to do with that, and you can't mix me up in it either."

"It's your whiskey, Hoak."

"It's been a long time since we've had a hanging in Tahlequah," said Delbert Swim.

Hoak sat silent for a moment, but he was getting nervous, and it showed.

"Hell, I only got this stuff this morning," he said finally. "Early this morning. I got it over in Missouri. I just got in here with it right before dark. I don't know nothing about them two bottles over there. If you've had them a couple of days, somebody else brought them in here. Not me."

"No one else has got any of this stuff,"

said George. "You're the only source. We've checked it all out. And that means that you're our only suspect in the murder."

"No. I ain't going to let you do this. I bought that whiskey from Matt Thomson. That's the truth. I paid Matt right here in Tahlequah. He gave me a note, and I took it up to Joe Carter to get the whiskey. Matt and Joe, they got a whole bunch of it stored up there in Joe's barn."

"Who is this Joe Carter?" said George. "Is he a Cherokee citizen?"

"No. Hell no. He's a white man. Lives in Missouri. Just across the line. His place and Matt's place comes together there at the line. They stored the whiskey at Joe's place because it's in Missouri. It's legal. That's where I got it, and that's the truth."

George stood up.

"It may be legal in Missouri, but just as soon as you bring it across that line you've broken the law. Come on, Hoak," he said.

"Where? Where we going?"

"Back to the cell. We're done with you for now."

Delbert Swim took Hoak by an arm and led him out of the office. Beehunter still sat there in the chair against the wall. George wished that he could speak some Cherokee or that Beehunter could understand a little English. He felt completely helpless. Just then Rider walked in. The sound of the door startled George.

160

"Rider," he said. "What are you doing back here?"

"I seen some activity down here from up on the bluff," said Rider. "I just come on back down here to ask you that same question." He glanced over at Beehunter. "What are you two doing here so late?"

Between the two of them in their two different languages, George and Beehunter filled Rider in on their evening's activities. Then Rider went upstairs to take a look at Hoak Fletcher in his cell and at the load of whiskey in the other cell. Hoak was pacing the floor. The three drunks were asleep. Back in the office Rider sat down behind his big desk.

"Well," he said, "the mystery of the missing whiskey-bottle label is solved. And I think the other one is, too. Just about. I think we for sure have enough now to arrest Matthew Thomson for the murder of Eli Martin. We just still don't know why he done it."

"And we have Thomson, Fletcher, and Carter for whiskey traffic," said George. "Except we can't cross the line to arrest Carter or to confiscate the whiskey."

"No," said Rider, "but Elwood Lovely can. First thing in the morning, George, I want you to send a wire to Elwood. I'll write out the message for you. I want you to send it for me, because I hope to be on the road to Delaware District by the time you can get it sent."

161

"Okay, Rider," said George.

Rider wrote out the message and handed it to George. Then he turned toward Beehunter.

"You did a good day's work today, my friend," he said in Cherokee. "But now we have another prisoner in here. Can you stay the night for me?"

Beehunter smiled. He knew at last that he was still trusted by Go-Ahead Rider.

"Yes, Go-Ahead," he said. "I can stay."

"Delbert," said Rider, "I appreciate your sticking around this late tonight. Now that Beehunter's back, you can run on home to your family."

Delbert Swim nodded as he reached for his hat.

"Thanks, Rider," he said.

Rider stopped by Judge Boley's office early the following morning. The judge was in and had the papers ready. Rider took them and left. He rode east out of Tahlequah until he reached the Illinois River. Then he turned north and followed the river up into Delaware District. It was evening by the time he reached the home of Captain Fish, the sheriff of Delaware District, near Olympus.

"Go-Ahead Rider," said Fish, speaking English and standing just outside his front door. "I haven't seen you for a long time. Put your horse away over there and come in."

Captain Fish's wife was a white woman named Sally. It was because of Sally that Captain Fish spoke English to Rider. Sally served Rider some beans and cornbread left over from their evening meal, and she made a fresh pot of coffee.

After finishing his meal, Rider thanked Sally, then filled his corncob pipe with tobacco from the pouch he carried in his vest pocket. He pulled out a wooden match and struck it on the bottom of the table and lit his pipe. Then he settled back to smoke and to drink one more cup of coffee. It had been a long ride from Tahlequah, and it felt good to sit back and relax.

"Now, Go-Ahead," said Captain Fish, "what brings you up here to these parts?"

"I've come with the intention of arresting one of your citizens," said Rider, and he produced the papers signed by Judge Boley and handed them to Fish. Fish gave them a quick study and laid them down on the table.

"So Matt Thomson killed Eli Martin in your jail, huh?" he said.

"I suppose I shouldn't say so until after the trial," said Rider, "but it sure looks that way. The evidence all points to him. And I have other evidence that he's started running whiskey into the Cherokee Nation with the help of his neighbor Joe Carter."

"I know Carter," said Fish. "He's no good,

too. I ain't too surprised by this. You know, Thomson ran for a council seat up here last time around. I sure am glad he never made it. He's been a shiftless, lazy scamp ever since I've knowed him. And that Carter, his neighbor across the line, he's just white trash. You might even say it's high time them two got hooked up together in something like this."

"Do you know whether or not Thomson has come back to Delaware District?" asked Rider.

"Didn't know he was gone. I haven't seen him for some time now," said Fish. "But we'll take a ride over to his place first thing in the morning and see what we can find out."

"Did you know Martin?"

"Not very well. I knew him when I saw him. That's about all. I did see him a while back, though. He was just getting ready to make a trip to St. Louis to negotiate a sale for some of the ranchers over in Cooweescoowee District."

"Did he make that trip?"

"I don't know. I assume that he did."

"The one thing I haven't been able to figure out, Cap," said Rider, "is why Thomson killed Martin. I can't even find any connection between them, but it was a deliberate, cold-blooded murder, carefully planned. I just don't know why."

"Joe," called Thomson. "Joe. Wake up and let me in. Joe. It's me. Matt Thomson. Wake up, Joe."

Joe Carter opened his front door while holding a gun in his right hand. He was rubbing his eyes with the back of his left.

"Matt? What the hell you doing here? God damn, it's the middle of the night. Do you know what time it is? I thought you was still in Tahlequah anyhow. I might have shot you. Hollering around like that in the middle of the night."

Thomson pushed his way past Carter and went on into the house. Carter shut the door and followed him, yawning and still rubbing his eyes. He put the pistol down on his table and dropped into a chair.

"Never mind all that," said Thomson. "We got a serious problem. I need a couple of men to do a job. Best they be white men. From over here in Missouri or down in Arkansas. You got to help me find them."

"What kind of job?" said Carter. "You told me there wouldn't be no problems with this deal. You said it was a perfect setup."

"Shut up and listen to me. What it is, is a killing job. I need to have a man killed. Right away. The sooner the better."

Carter leaned back heavily in his chair, a stunned look on his face. His bleary eyes at last opened wide, and his mouth hung open for a moment.

"I don't know no killers," he said. "What do you take me for anyway? I don't know no killers, and I don't want nothing to do with no killings either. Not me. No sir. Running whiskey into Indian territory, that's one thing. But killing, that's something else altogether."

"Oh yeah?" said Thomson. "Well, you better have something to do with this one, because if we don't get it done right away, we'll both wind up in jail at least. We might both hang for murder."

"What do you mean both hang for murder? How can we hang for murder if we don't do no killing? Just what the hell are you talking about anyway?"

"Listen," said Thomson, "and listen good. While I was in St. Louis meeting with Palmer to set up this deal, Eli Martin come walking in the place and saw me. He saw me there with Palmer. I couldn't take no chances on Martin saying anything that would connect me with Palmer. Not with what we were fixing to get into here. There was too much at stake. You see?"

"Yeah?"

"So I killed him."

"You killed him? Martin? Just like that?"

"Well, not just like that, but I did it, and that's all that counts right now."

"And you never bothered to tell me all that, did you? You just let me come in on this here deal with you just like everything was all right. I knew I shouldn't get mixed up in no business deal with no Indian. I just knew it."

"I didn't tell you because I knew you'd start acting like this," said Thomson. "Besides that, I thought I had it covered up real good, and I did, too, but Go-Ahead Rider figured it all out somehow, and he's after me now. And by God, if he gets me, he'll get you, too. And even if I was to tell him the truth, you know how the laws are. You're in the whiskey business with me. They'll figure you was in on the killing, too."

Carter shoved back his chair and stood up. He paced across the floor and back again. Then he suddenly picked up the pistol from his table top and pointed it with a shaking hand toward Thomson's chest.

"Damn you, Matt," he said. "I ought to kill you. You should have told me all about this before. You didn't have no right to get me involved in no killing like that."

"Well, it's done," said Thomson, "and now we have to stop Go-Ahead Rider. You have to help me find somebody who can do it. Now put down that six-gun before you hurt one of us, and sit back down here, and let's figure this thing out, real calm and sensible like."

Chapter 16

"He's been here, Cap," said Rider. He had just opened the valise he found sitting on the floor beside the bed, and he pulled the Rupertus pocket pistol out of it. "I'd bet a month's pay that this right here's the gun that killed Eli Martin."

Captain Fish walked over to look at the gun. Rider was holding it up in the sunlight that was streaming in through the window. He squinted and turned the gun this way and that. Then he held it over for Captain Fish to get a better look.

"I'll bet that's buffalo hair on there too," he said. "Matt Thomson's my man, all right. All I've got to do is find him."

"Well," said Captain Fish, "he came home, but he's gone again. I sure don't know where to look next. I guess we can put out posters on him. Not much else we can do."

"He might be over at his partner's house," said Rider.

"But we can't go over there. Not officially."

"No," said Rider. "We'll have to wait for

168

Elwood for that. Let's look around here a little more."

"For what? You've got all the evidence you need to convict him of the murder."

"I'd still like to know why he did it," said Rider. "And I do have this search warrant. I ought to use it while I've got it."

Captain Fish gave a shrug and looked around. He walked over to the table. There were some dirty dishes there, and some paper and a pencil stub. The paper was all blank. He started to walk away and look elsewhere, hesitated, then picked up the folded newspaper that was also there on the table.

"Hey, Rider," he said.

"What?"

"Look at this."

He held up the paper as Rider walked toward him.

"It's the *St. Louis Democrat.*"

Rider's eyes lit up.

"What date?" he asked.

Captain Fish unfolded the paper to search for the date, and by then Rider was looking over his shoulder. Both men spoke almost together.

"August twelfth."

"Cap," said Rider, "do you think that you could find a way to confirm whether or not Eli Martin actually made that trip to St. Louis, and if so, what dates he was there?"

"Yeah, Go-Ahead," said Captain Fish. "I think I can do that."

"This just might be the first thing we have to make any kind of connection between the two men — other than the killing itself."

"Well, then, have you got enough?"

"I'm going to look around a little more, Cap. You can go on back if you want to. In fact, you'd be more help to me now if you was to go on and check into Martin's St. Louis trip. I can finish up here all right."

"You sure?"

"I'm sure."

"Stop back by my place when you're done."

Captain Fish left Rider alone at Thomson's house, and Rider went into the bedroom again. He had found the valise in there, but he had not bothered yet to search further. He decided to open drawers, to look at everything.

In the fourth drawer he opened he found the buffalo mitten, the mate to the one back in his office, the one through which the fatal shot had been fired. For someone who so carefully planned a killing, thought Rider, Thomson made some stupid mistakes. He probably thought that his scheme was so clever that no one would ever figure it out, but he should have got rid of that cane pole, and he should have got rid of the pistol and this other glove. He dropped that one glove back there in Tahlequah, and apparently never knew it, or never thought it was important. And he should have burned this newspaper.

170

No, he ain't nearly as smart as he thinks he is.

Rider put the newspaper, the mitten, and the pistol on the table. His case was almost complete. He still wanted to know more about the St. Louis trip. Had Eli Martin and Matt Thomson been in St. Louis at the same time? Had they met there? If so, had it been by design or by accident? Was it possible even that they had gone to St. Louis together?

It was somewhere around noon, judging from the position of the sun in the sky, when Rider decided to abandon his search. He had nothing more. He had the newspaper, the pistol, and the mitten. That would have to do until he could find Thomson himself or until Elwood Lovely arrived with his authority as a deputy United States marshal, and they could go across the state line onto the property of Joe Carter.

Rider decided to go on back to Captain Fish's house to wait for Lovely. As he opened the front door and stepped out, the mitten, pistol, and newspaper in his hand, a shot rang out, and a bullet smacked into the door frame just by his head.

Rider jumped back inside and slammed the door. He dropped his evidence on the floor just inside the door and pulled one of his Colts out of his waistband. The shot had come from somewhere out front, somewhere

171

more or less in front of the house. Rider tried to recall the lay of the land.

There was a long lane that ran from the house out to the main road. The road had been cut through heavy timber and was still lined on both sides with trees and thick brush. But where the lane turned off from the road to go to Thomson's house, the trees began to thin out. Thomson's house was in the middle of a large clearing. Rider figured the shooter was probably at the edge of the lane up near the road, hidden in the trees.

Rider sidled up to a front window to try to get a look out in that direction. He could see the trees to the left side of the lane way out there by the road, but he couldn't see anyone lurking about in them. He ducked down to go beneath the window and moved to the other side of the door. There was another window over there.

He edged up to that window and peered out again. This time he could see the trees on the right side of the lane. Still he saw no sign of a hidden gunman. The shot had to have come from the trees, he thought. And then, I'm caught in a trap.

The distance from the house to the trees was too great for his Colts to be of any use, but it was an easy rifle shot. The man in the trees had a rifle. Rider's rifle was outside on his horse. He thought about making a run for it, but quickly discarded that idea as dangerously foolish.

If the shooter in the trees was a halfway good shot, he could get Rider before Rider could get the rifle out of the boot. And even if he did manage to get to the rifle without getting shot in the process, he wouldn't know where to point it. He had not so far been able to locate the shooter.

He'd just have to wait the man out, he decided, but then, how long would he wait? If he stayed inside and didn't present a target, and the shooter didn't shoot again, how would he know whether or not the man had given up and gone away? But then, maybe he should give the man a target. Get him to shoot again. But to what purpose? If he did manage to spot the man, he wouldn't be able to compete with him at that range. No. The thing to do was to get the man to think that he had accomplished his purpose.

Rider looked around the room, and there in a front corner stood a homemade coat rack, a pole about the height of a man, mounted on a stand. Toward the top end were three short pieces set into the pole to be used as hooks for coats or hats. That should do the trick. He recalled having seen a jacket thrown on the bedroom floor, and he went in there to get it.

Back in the main room, Rider draped the

jacket across two of the hooks. Then he took off his hat and placed it on top of the pole. He moved the dressed up coat rack to the wall just beside one of the front windows. The idea was to push the rack out in front of the window enough to give the shooter the outline of a man to shoot at, and to let him think that he had hit his mark.

He took a deep breath and pushed the rack forward, not too much, just enough to make it look as if he was peering around the corner. There was another shot and another. There were two rifles. Two shooters. One shot went a little wide. The other smashed into the pole just below the hat. Then a third shot rang out, and the bullet tore through the jacket.

The pole rocked a bit from the one solid hit it had taken, but it still stood. Rider reached out cautiously and gave it a shove. It fell forward. Everything was quiet. Rider waited there beside the door, pressed against the wall, a Colt in his right hand, the hammer thumbed back. They would come to make sure the job was finished.

It seemed like an incredibly long wait, but Rider figured that the two men would not immediately start for the house. They would wait a bit to see whether or not their victim got up again. Then they would start for the house slowly, probably spread out wide just in case he were to step out the door or pop up in a window ready to shoot. He waited.

Then he thought that he could hear soft footsteps. They were moving in slowly and carefully. They weren't quite fools. He wondered if they were Thomson and Carter. He couldn't imagine anyone else they could be. The footsteps came closer, and Rider was sure then that they were footsteps.

Then there was a push to the door from the outside, and the door began to move inward slowly, and it creaked as it moved. Rider saw the hand that was pushing it. Then the hand was withdrawn, and the door stood wide open. Rider waited.

Then the man stepped inside. He was holding a rifle ready, and he didn't see Rider at first. Then he saw him there to his left, and he turned fast, raising the rifle as he turned, and Rider pulled the trigger of his Colt. The .38 made a loud explosion there inside the small room, and it opened a dark hole in the rifleman's chest. The man made only a small noise, as if he had been punched in the stomach. His face took on an expression of both shock and surprise. He stood for a moment weaving, then he fell on his face — dead.

Rider went quickly out the front door, and he spotted the other rifleman at once. The man was about ten paces out from the house and off to Rider's right. Rider fired and missed. The man raised his rifle to his shoulder, and Rider fired again. His second bullet ripped into the man's thigh, and the man screamed in pain and dropped his rifle.

"Don't kill me," he said. "Look. I dropped my gun. Don't shoot me again. I quit. I give up."

Rider marveled at how a man who would so casually shoot another would whimper when his own time came. He sneered at the man.

"Move away from that rifle," he said.

The man moved sideways, dragging his shot leg, groaning and whimpering with each move he made.

"Why did you try to kill me?" said Rider.

"It was a mistake. We thought you was somebody else."

"Are you a Cherokee citizen?" Rider asked.

"Who? Me? Hell no. I'm pure white from Missouri."

"All right, white man," said Rider, "let me explain something to you. Your government won't let me arrest you. If I take you in, I have to get ahold of a U.S. marshal, and I have to do a lot of paperwork. You cause me a whole lot of trouble — alive. But I can kill you in self-defense. I can do that. Then I don't have so much trouble. You understand me?"

"Yes. I think so. I ain't going to lie to you. Don't kill me."

"What's your name?"

"Lonnie Jenkins."

"And your buddy inside there. Who's he?"

"His name's Charlie Polk. Charlie Polk. Is he dead?"

"I didn't have time not to kill him," said Rider. "Now one more time, for the last time, why were you two gunning for me?"

"We was paid."

"How much am I worth?"

"Fifty dollars."

"And who paid you, Mr. Jenkins?"

Jenkins looked down at the ground in front of his feet.

"My leg hurts, mister," he said. "I'm bleeding real bad. Can't you do something to stop the bleeding and then get me a doctor?"

"If you don't answer my questions pretty quick, you just might bleed to death standing there," said Rider. "Or I might get tired of waiting for you to die and just shoot you again to put you out of your misery. I'd do that much for a dog. I guess I could do it for you."

"Please, mister. You're a lawman."

"Who paid you?"

"Joe Carter. Joe Carter paid us."

"Was Carter alone?"

"No. There was another man. I didn't know him. I can't remember his name. Honest."

"That ain't good enough, Mr. Jenkins," said Rider. He raised his Colt and pointed it at Jenkins's chest.

"It's the honest-to-God truth," Jenkins screamed. "I can't recall the man's name. This here's his house, though."

"You sure about that?"

"Yes. Yes. This is his house right here. He told us you was here. He watched you earlier. You come out here with another man, and then the other man left. Then he come on over to Joe's place and got us. He said you was here all by yourself, and now was the time for us to do it."

"Did you and Polk bring horses out here?" Rider asked.

"They're out there in the road," said Jenkins, "beyond them trees."

Rider walked over to his own horse and climbed into the saddle. He turned the horse toward the road.

"All right," he said. "Let's go."

"I can't walk all the way out there," whined Jenkins.

"Then you'll die right here," said Rider, and Jenkins turned and started walking toward the road.

Chapter 17

George Tanner was bored. He guessed that Rider had meant it when he said that he needed George to stay in Tahlequah and be in charge of things. Someone had to be in charge, and who else did Rider have? George was his only full-time deputy. Still he couldn't help feeling that he was being left out of the important events, certainly the exciting ones. Nothing was really happening in Tahlequah, nothing of any significance. Nothing but routine. There had been a few more drunk-and-disorderlies to lock up, but that had been expected with so many people in town for the council meeting. But George would much rather have gone out with Rider to help round up Thomson and Carter.

He had sent the message to Deputy United States Marshal Elwood Lovely as Rider had instructed him to do, and since then there had been nothing. Nothing except making sure all the special deputies were on duty around the capitol building and patrolling the streets for drunks. And in spite of the number of people in Tahlequah for the council meeting, and the few arrests, things had seemed remarkably quiet. Perhaps the news of the killing in the jail and the extensive investigation and manhunt had scared some folks out of any public rowdy behavior. Or perhaps things only seemed quiet to George, because arresting drunks was quiet compared to hunting killers. Anyhow, George was bored.

It was about noon when he walked over to the capitol square and found Earl Bob. He told the special deputy to take off for lunch.

"Take your time," he said. "There's nothing happening around here. I'll stay till you get back."

Waiting for Earl Bob's return, George wondered if he had made the right decision when he had agreed to be Go-Ahead Rider's deputy. He had been educated at Harvard in the classics, and he had thought that when he returned home to the Cherokee Nation, he would find himself a job as a teacher. Instead Rider had offered him this deputy's job, and he had taken it. There were times when it was interesting, fascinating even, but mostly it was dull routine.

He wondered if teaching, too, would get to be that way after a while. Probably it would, but he decided that he'd ask Lee about that. She didn't seem to be bored with teaching, not ever. That thought caused him to muse for a bit on the charms of his wife and his own incredible luck at finding such a woman for himself. But soon enough his thoughts moved back on track.

Perhaps it was the potential for adventure that kept him with Rider, he thought, and then he realized how he had formed that thought. He had thought "with Rider." And George knew that the reason he stayed with the deputy's job was not so much because of the job as it was because of Rider, because of the force of the man's personality, because of the things he could learn from Rider, because he loved being associated with Rider. Some of the reputation of Rider rubbed off on everyone who worked for him, worked with him. And that was important to George.

Go-Ahead Rider was a hero of the Civil War in Indian territory, a captain in the Indian Home Guard. After the war he had become a law-enforcement officer, and his reputation for bravery and honesty and fairness had only increased since then. Yes, George admitted to himself, likely it was for the prestige of being known as Go-Ahead Rider's deputy that he stayed with his job.

Earl Bob returned after only about a half an hour, and he walked over to where George waited.

"Thanks," he said. "Your wife's down there. Why don't you go get some lunch? There's plenty good food. I didn't eat it all up from you."

"Yeah," said George. "I think I'll just do that."

He walked across the square and then across Water Street. Soon he was at the campsite of Earl Bob's family. He kissed his wife on the cheek and nodded a greeting to the others. Earl Bob's family were all there, as were Rider's. George sat down, and Lee began heaping up a plate for him. Akie poured him a cup of coffee.

"Thanks," said George. *Wado.*"

"Jali," said Buster, "do you like the fish?"

"Yeah," said George. "It's good. Real good."

"We caught them," said Jali.

"You did?" said George. "Really?"

"Yeah," said Buster. "With Daddy's fishing poles."

"All of them? Just you two boys?"

"We caught them all," said Buster.

"Every one," added Jali.

"Well, you're getting to be pretty big boys, I guess. I had no idea you two were getting to be such good fishermen, though."

"Well, we are," said Buster.

"We're the best," said Jali. "And you know why?"

"No," said George. "Why are you the best?"

"Because we're full-bloods."

"Oh," said George. "Well, maybe you're right about that."

"Jali," said Akie, her voice scolding.

"Who cleaned them?" asked George. "The

182

fish. Who cleaned them?"

The boys were quiet for a moment. They looked at each other. Then Buster answered.

"Our mamas did," he said.

George finished his lunch and complimented the ladies on the cooking. He also praised the fishermen once again. He was about to leave to go back to work when Lee stopped him.

"George?" she said.

"Yes?"

"Can you wait a minute?"

"Yeah. Sure. What is it?"

"Well, this really isn't the way I planned to tell you, but these ladies here figured it out for themselves, so you're the only one here who doesn't know."

George waited a moment. When Lee didn't say anything more, he said, "Doesn't know what?"

"Let's walk over this way, George," said Lee, taking George by the arm.

"Lee," he said, "what's this all about?"

She led him away from the others, over into the area where Thomson had camped for the one night. Buster and Jali started to run after them, but Akie and Exie both called the boys back.

"Lee?" said George, a little aggravation in his voice.

"George, there's going to be three of us."

"Three of us where? Us who?"

"Three of us Tanners in our house, George," she said.

"What? You mean that you — We — A baby?"

"Yes, George. A baby."

"Are — Are you sure?"

"I'm sure."

"Oh. Oh. You should be home. You shouldn't be out like this. Wait. You can't walk all that way. I'll go get a buggy and be right back for you. You just sit down over here and wait for me. I'll be right back."

"George," said Lee.

"What?"

"I'm just fine, and I don't want to go home yet. And when I'm ready to go home, I can walk. It's not all that far."

"But you —"

"George, I want to spend the day here with our friends. If it will make you feel any better, when it's time for you to quit work for the day, you can get a buggy and come for me then. All right?"

"Well, all right. If you're sure."

"I'm sure, George. Now go on back to work."

"Okay," said George. He turned and started to walk back toward the capitol building.

"George?" said Lee.

"Yes?"

"I love you."

"I love you," said George.

Back on the capitol square, George ran over to where Earl Bob was standing.

"I'm going to be a daddy," he said, a big grin spreading across his face.

"I know," said Earl Bob.

"You know?"

"They were talking about it down there, the women."

Walking back toward the jail, George grumbled to himself.

"I'm the last one to know," he said. "I wonder if Rider knows already. Beehunter probably knows. Maybe even Judge Boley. The whole damned national council. Maybe they even discussed it in the general session this morning."

But even as he grumbled, he smiled, a wide smile that stretched his lips.

"We were just about to come looking for you," said Elwood Lovely, as Rider rode up to Captain Fish's house. "Looks like you didn't need any help, though."

Rider was leading two horses. On one Lonnie Jenkins sat, his bloody leg wrapped around with a dirty bandanna. Across the saddle of the other the body of Charlie Polk was slung.

"I'm glad you're here, Elwood," said Rider. "I really can't arrest these two. Well, this one. But they started shooting at me from ambush."

185

"Well, you just write me out a report," said Lovely, "and I'll take them from there." He walked over to the horse on which Jenkins sat. "Howdy, Lonnie," he said. "I knew I'd be getting you sooner or later, one way or another."

"So you know this one," said Rider.

"That's been my misfortune, Rider. Who's the other one?"

Rather than wait for an answer to his question, Lovely stepped over to the dangling body and lifted the head by its hair in order to take a look.

"It's Charlie," said Jenkins, the whimper still in his voice. "That goddamned Indian killed him. No reason. He just killed him."

"Oh, shut up, Lonnie," said Lovely. "Cap, have you got anyplace to lock this pissant up in?"

"I can find a place," said Captain Fish.

"I need a doctor," said Jenkins.

"Shut up," said Lovely.

Captain Fish took Jenkins's horse by the reins and started to lead him off.

"Come on," he said. "I'll take real good care of you till Woody's ready to take you in."

"Rider," said Lovely, "you ready to fill me in on what's going on here?"

"Elwood," said Rider, "I'm after a man named Matthew Thomson for the murder of Eli Martin. In the course of my investigation,

186

I discovered that Thomson was running whiskey into the Cherokee Nation with the help of a white man named Joe Carter."

"I know Carter," said Lovely. "I'm not surprised to hear that about him. Go on."

"Well, he's the reason I wanted you in on this. My information tells me that the whiskey's stored over in Carter's barn on the Missouri side of the line.

"I didn't know anything about these other two, Jenkins and Polk, till they started shooting at me, but Jenkins told me that it was Carter and Thomson who hired them to kill me.

"I've got it all pinned down except for one thing, and that is, why did Thomson kill Martin in the first place? That's the part that I still can't figure out. But it looks like they might have been in St. Louis at the same time, shortly before the murder, which, by the way, took place right in my jail."

Lovely asked Rider questions until he had all the details filled in. Just about then, Captain Fish returned.

"I've got your boy in a safe place, Woody," he said.

"Thanks, Cap. I may need to leave him there for a while, till we get this business of Rider's all cleared up."

"By the way, Cap," said Rider, "were you able to find out anything more about Martin's trip to St. Louis?"

"He was there the same time as Thomson,"

said Captain Fish. "At least, he was there the same time as the date on that newspaper we found at Thomson's house. I can't confirm that Thomson went, though."

"We can do that at Seneca," said Lovely. "I might even be able to get some information out of St. Louis about the movements of both men while they were there."

"That would be a big help, Elwood," said Rider.

"Well, then," said Lovely, "what now?"

"If me and Cap here can ride along with you," said Rider, "unofficially, of course, I think it might be a good idea to pay a visit to old Joe Carter's place."

"I kind of thought you might say that. Well, I'm ready if you are."

"Cap?" said Rider.

"Just let me tell my old lady and saddle my horse," said Captain Fish, "and I'll be right along."

Chapter 18

"Those two ought to be getting back by now, don't you think?" asked Thomson. "They've had plenty of time to get the job done by now. More than enough."

"It all depends, Matt. Here. Have another drink. This really is good whiskey. I got to hand it to you for that. You sure do know how to pick good whiskey."

"Depends on what? What are you talking about?"

"Huh? Oh. Well," said Carter, pouring the last of the whiskey into their two glasses, "if they meant to wait in them trees where we left them until Rider come out of the house on his own and then to just pick him off, maybe they had a longer wait than what we expected. Hell, maybe they're still waiting."

"Ah, what the hell could Rider do in my house for such a long time as this? Tell me that. There ain't nothing in there for him to look at. They ought to be getting back over here. They ought to have done it already. That's what I know."

Carter looked thoughtful for a moment, his face registering something very close to pain.

"Matt?" he said.

"What?"

"What if something did go wrong? What if them lawmen did get them two, and then they come over here after us?"

"In the first place, you dumb bastard," said Thomson, "Captain Fish already left. He was watching. Remember? So if by some miracle Rider was to get past those two — number one, he's by himself. Number two, he can't do anything over here anyhow. It's out of his jurisdiction."

"Oh, yeah. Well then, how come you're worrying so much? What are you so nervous about?"

"Nothing," Thomson snapped irritably. He tipped up his glass and took another drink. "It's just that they ought to be back. That's all." He drained his glass and set it back down on the table with a thump. "Pour me another," he said, "will you?"

"This here bottle's empty, Matt," said Carter. "We got plenty more, though. You want me to go out in the barn and get another one? I'll go get another one."

"No. Never mind," said Thomson. "I'll go get it myself. I'm tired of just sitting around here anyway. I need to get up and do something. I'll go. Hell."

Thomson left the house and headed for the

barn. He was staggering just a bit. He and Carter hadn't consumed the whole bottle that day, but they had drunk enough. He felt unsteady on his feet, slightly woozy. He stopped a moment, stood still and took a few deep breaths. Then he went on, but more slowly and carefully. When he reached the big barn door, he hesitated again, leaning heavily against it. Then he lifted the bar, tossed it aside and dragged the door open wide, stumbling and almost falling in the process.

Inside the barn he found a bottle, grabbed it by the neck, and turned to go back out. He paused for just a second in slightly muddled thought, then turned back and grabbed another bottle in his other hand. He made his way back to the door and was about to walk outside and head back toward the house when he saw the three riders coming down the road. He stopped and stared, squinting his eyes against the sun.

Three riders? There should only be two. He rubbed his eyes with a forearm, and strained to see. The riders came closer. Their forms became clearer. Then he realized with a start that the two killers he had hired were not among them, and then he recognized Captain Fish, and then Go-Ahead Rider. He did not know the third man.

But Rider and Fish. What were they doing here? On Carter's farm? In Missouri? They were outside of their jurisdiction. They had no business here. Did they have no respect for the law? Should he confront them? Tell them to get out? Or did they want him so badly that they would ignore the jurisdictional problem and attack him anyway? Make outlaws of themselves? Try to drag him back across the line by force? Kill him even? Or — another bad thought — could the third man be a Missouri lawman or a federal one?

Thomson had no gun, so his choices were severely limited. If he did not confront the Cherokee lawmen with the jurisdictional issue, then what could he do? Run or hide. There were no other possibilities that he could come up with. And if he did do one of those two things, run or hide, then what would Carter do?

He decided that Carter would have to worry about Carter. This was no time to be concerned with what that fool might do. This was a crisis. It would have to be every man for himself. Let Carter cover his own ass. He dropped the two bottles of whiskey where he stood, turned and went through the barn to the back door, opened it, and ran for the woods.

Joe Carter fired a rifle through his front window, and the three lawmen reined in their mounts. Captain Fish pulled a Winchester out of a saddle boot.

"Hold it, Cap," said Elwood Lovely. "If

that's Joe Carter in there, I think he shot wide on purpose. Just a kind of a warning shot. He ain't hardly brave enough to fight."

"All right," said Captain Fish, but he held the rifle ready.

"Joe," shouted Lovely. "Joe Carter. Is that you in there?"

"Well, of course it's me," yelled Carter. "This is my house here, ain't it? Who else would it be in my own house shooting at trespassers?"

"Joe, this is Elwood Lovely talking. You know me, and you know that I ain't no trespasser."

"I know it. I know who you are."

"All right, then put down your rifle and come on out here and talk to us. We don't want to shoot you. We didn't come here for that."

"I don't have to go out of my own house and talk to no Indian lawmen," said Carter. "I know enough for that. They ain't got no jury diction over here."

"They're not here to arrest you," said Lovely. "We came for a talk."

"That's all?"

"That's all, Joe, for right now."

"You ain't going to let them two take me back across the line, are you?"

"I couldn't do that if I wanted to," said Lovely. "That's against the law. Now put down the rifle and come on out here."

"That one Indian," said Carter, "he's holding a rifle."

"That's because you shot at us, Joe. You put your rifle down and step out the door, and he'll put his rifle away."

There was a pause, then the door slowly opened. Joe Carter, with an obsequious step, came out onto his front stoop. He was unarmed. Lovely gave Captain Fish a look, and Fish put his rifle away. Then the three lawmen rode slowly toward Carter.

"I didn't really try to hit none of y'all," said Carter. "I can shoot better than that."

"I know, Joe," said Lovely. The lawmen had reached the porch by then. They reined in and dismounted. Carter looked nervously from one to another.

"What y'all want with me?" he said. "I ain't done nothing. I ain't broke no laws."

"Well, we don't know about that," said Lovely, "but we do think you might have some information that we're looking for."

"Well, then, what can I do for you? I'm always happy to help out the law any way I can."

"Joe," said Lovely, "do you know a man named Matthew Thomson?"

"Well, sure I know him. He's my next neighbor. He lives just across the line into the Indian territory. The Cherokee Nation. You know."

"Did you recently enter into a business venture with Thomson?"

"What do you mean?"

"Did you and Thomson become partners in a business deal?"

"It's all legal," said Carter. "I ain't broke no laws."

"Have you got whiskey stored in your barn?" asked Rider.

"I can go get a warrant," said Lovely. "Are you going to make me do that?"

"No, hell, I ain't going to make you do that. It's out there. But it ain't against the law. Not here."

"It's against the law if you sell it across the line," said Captain Fish.

"Well, I never. I only sold it once so far, and I sold it right here on my own land. Right here. I don't know where the man who bought it took it from here. That ain't none of my business. If somebody bought whiskey from me and then took it over there, that ain't my fault."

"All right," said Lovely, "calm down. We're not accusing you. We're asking you."

"Do you know where Matt Thomson is at, Mr. Carter?" asked Rider.

Carter's fidgeting became worse, and he glanced toward the barn.

"Is he out there?" said Lovely.

"Maybe you better go get that there warrant, Elwood," said Carter. "I ain't going to say nothing else."

"Carter," said Rider, "Matthew Thomson is a Cherokee citizen, and he's wanted in the

195

Cherokee Nation for murder, attempted murder, and whiskey running. Now we don't know if you're an accomplice or not, but if you try to cover up for him, you'll sure make it look that way."

"That ain't got nothing to do with Missouri," said Carter. "I know that much."

"Joe," said Lovely, "if you and Thomson went into this whiskey business intending to introduce it into the Indian territory, then you violated the laws of the United States. If you and Thomson hired killers in Missouri to cross the line and do a murder, then you're in violation of a federal law."

"We can't arrest you," said Rider, nodding toward Lovely, "but he can."

"Joe, the best thing for you to do is cooperate," said Lovely. "Maybe you didn't know that Thomson was going to sell that whiskey across the line. Maybe you didn't know that he hired those killers."

Rider knew that Carter had been with Thomson when the killers were hired. Carter's had been the name that Jenkins had mentioned. He had said that he didn't know the other man's name, only his house. But Rider knew that Lovely was trying to draw some information out of Carter. He might even let Carter get away with proclaiming his innocence through ignorance of his partner's actions in order to get Thomson. Thomson was the bigger fish, he was the schemer.

Carter was a dupe.

"Well, you're right about that, Elwood," said Carter. "Really, the business is all Matt's. He just said that whiskey was illegal over there, so he needed to do business over here. He needed to use my barn for storing the stuff. I just let him do it. That's all."

"What about the hired killers, Polk and Jenkins?" asked Rider.

"I don't know nothing about that."

"Is Thomson in your barn?" said Lovely.

"He was in the house with me, drinking," said Carter, and he heaved a heavy sigh. "We run out, and he went out there to get another bottle. That was just before you all come riding up. He must have seen you."

Lovely looked at Rider and Captain Fish.

"You two want to check it out?" he said.

Rider looked at Fish. "Let's go," he said, and the two district sheriffs headed for the barn.

"Be careful," Lovely called out after them. Then he turned back toward Carter. "Joe," he said, "it looks like Thomson killed a man in Tahlequah, a man named Eli Martin. Killed him right in the jailhouse there. Do you know anything about that?"

Carter's head was hanging low. He didn't bother looking up when he answered.

"He told me," he said.

"Do you know why Thomson killed Martin?"

"Martin seen him in St. Louis talking with the whiskey man."

"The whiskey man? You mean the supplier? The man he bought the whiskey from?"

"Yeah. Him. I think his name was Palmer."

"Joe, I'm going to ask you to go with me to my office and tell this whole story all over again so I can get it down on paper and get you to sign it. Are you willing to do that?"

Carter glanced toward the barn. Rider and Fish had gone inside. No shots sounded. He wondered if that meant that Thomson had got away. What would Thomson do to him for talking to Elwood Lovely?

"Yeah," he said. "I'll go. Be glad to, Elwood."

The two sheriffs reappeared and walked back over to join Lovely.

"Looks like he dropped the whiskey and run," said Captain Fish.

"There's nothing back there but woods," said Rider. "There's no telling where he went."

"Damn," said Elwood Lovely.

Chapter
19

Matthew Thomson ran through the woods until he was exhausted. He dropped to his knees, gasping for breath. It had been a long time since he had run so hard and so far, and he felt a pain in his chest. He cried out loud both from the pain and over his general misery at all his careful plans having been thwarted by Go-Ahead Rider. Then he fell forward on his face. He lay there until his breathing became easier again, and then he slept.

When he woke up again, it was dark, and he had no idea what time it was. He did not know what to do. He stood up and looked around himself, but he was deep in the woods. Other than that, he did not know exactly where he was. He had run out the back door of Joe Carter's barn and into the woods from there, and then he had just kept running. So he was somewhere in the woods in back of Carter's barn, but the woods there were extensive, and they did not stop at the edge of Carter's property.

He was probably, he thought, in Missouri

still, but it was even possible that he had inadvertently turned back west and crossed again into the Cherokee Nation. If he had done that, he would be back on his own property. He wasn't at all sure that he wanted to be back on his own property. Over there Rider or Fish either one could arrest him.

"The bastards," he said out loud.

But who the hell was that third man? If the Cherokee lawmen had enlisted the aid of a federal lawman, then there was no place safe. They could arrest him anywhere. He couldn't think straight. He needed some rest. He needed some food. He wanted a change of clothes. And he couldn't think of any place he could go for any of those things except his own house or Carter's house. He wondered if the lawmen would be watching those places. He decided to sneak back and have a look. He picked a direction that he thought would take him back to Carter's, and he started walking.

"You mean he got away? Clean?" said George.

"Well, George, we'll get him sooner or later. Elwood done everything he could, and we were out of our jurisdiction," said Rider. He poured himself a cup of coffee and took it over to his desk. "There'll be federal dodgers out on him as well as our own. He can't hide forever."

"That just really peeves me," said George. "First the man commits a murder right here in our jail, and he makes it look as if Beehunter had done it. He made me suspect Beehunter. He made a fool out of me, Rider."

"Don't be so hard on yourself, George. Just about everybody thought Beehunter was guilty."

"Yeah. Everyone but you."

"I've known Beehunter all my life," said Rider. "I was practically raised with him."

"And then he actually paid two men to kill you."

"Yeah, well, one of them's dead and the other one'll most likely hang over at Fort Smith."

Rider took a sip of the coffee, then leaned back and put his feet on the desk. He pulled his pipe and tobacco pouch out and started to fill his pipe. George wondered how Rider could be taking all this so calmly.

"And what about Carter?" he said. "Is he going to get out of all this scot-free?"

"Well, he might, but then, I wouldn't worry too much about that. Carter ain't too bright, and I guess old Thomson just gave him a good line of talk. He most likely knew that Thomson intended to sell that whiskey in the Cherokee Nation, and he was almost for sure with Thomson when they hired them killers. But he ain't important. What we got from him in exchange for allowing him to get off was all the information we needed to fill in the gaps about Thomson. I'm satisfied with that."

"Immunity," said George.

"What's that?" said Rider.

"That's what Carter got. Immunity."

"Is that what you call it at Harvard? Well, that's all right. He wouldn't have been ours anyhow. Anything he done, he done it in Missouri, and he's a white man."

"Well, I don't like it, Rider. I don't like it a bit."

"George, one of the hardest things to learn about this business we're in is that you can't win them all. And when you lose, you got to take it as well as when you win. Otherwise you won't last long."

George sat down behind his desk across the room from Rider. He leaned back, looked up at the ceiling, took a deep breath, and exhaled long and loud.

"Rider," he said, "I don't know how you do it. No matter how long I stay with this job, I'll never be able to handle things the way you do."

Thomson had waited at the edge of the woods, lurking, watching, for a long time. He did not know how long. At last he had decided that there was no one at Carter's house, and he had run to the back door and gone inside. He found some hardtack and some jerky and a tin of beans, and he ate.

Then he found some clothes of Carter's that he could wear, and he changed. He felt a little better. He sat alone thinking. Only a few days ago, he had thought that he was well on his way to riches. Now he had nothing, and he was a fugitive. He had nothing, and he had nothing to look forward to. He could run away to Texas or California, and he could change his name and start all over again.

But what would he do? Find some kind of job? Doing what? He had no capital for investment. He had no particular skills. He certainly had no predilection to hard work. He was ruined.

He was ruined, and it was all the fault of Go-Ahead Rider. Then something marvelous happened to Matthew Thomson. He no longer felt sorry for himself. He no longer thought about wealth, or lost wealth. He no longer dreamed of a political future. He ceased being concerned about his own safety or even his own life.

He thought only of Go-Ahead Rider. He felt a renewed energy and renewed determination, and all was focused clearly and directly on Go-Ahead Rider. Now Matthew Thomson wanted only one thing more from life, and if he could accomplish that one thing, he would die content, if not happy. One thing only was left to do. He was possessed of a powerful need to kill Go-Ahead Rider.

He looked around the room, and he saw Carter's shotgun leaning against the wall beside the door. He ran to it and checked it. It was loaded. He searched the room until he found more shells, and he stuffed them in his pocket. Then he found a burlap sack, and he filled it with food. He would need his energy.

He ran out the back door and out to the barn where he was thrilled to find the horses still in their stalls. He saddled a horse, tied on the sack, and mounted up. He rode the horse out of the barn and down the lane to the main road, and then he headed south — toward Tahlequah.

George and Lee sat with the Riders in the dog run between the two log cabins that the Riders called home. They had just finished their evening meal. Exie had thought that, to help celebrate the good news of Lee's condition, they should have the Tanners over for supper. And the meal had been delicious. Everyone had overindulged. There had been chicken and dumplings, corn and beans, greens and sweet potatoes. And they had run out of nothing.

"Have some more," Exie had kept saying to George, because he was a man, and to Lee because she was "eating for two."

"Exie," Rider had said, "you've outdone yourself this time."

When Exie and Lee went back inside to clean up from the meal, and the kids were running around the yard, George and Rider sat alone in the dog run. Rider was smoking his pipe. Both men were relaxed, not only because of the big meal, but also because the council had adjourned that day, and things in Tahlequah were getting back to normal. The gray pup appeared in the dog run and made itself at home there beside Rider's chair. George gave it a scowl.

"What did the council ever do about the six million acres?" George asked. "Did you hear?"

"Oh, they finally directed the chief to write a letter of protest."

"You think they'll stop the sale?"

"No, but they might get a little more money out of it. That's all they'll get. If they get that."

There was a moment of silence, during which Rider reached down to scratch the pup between its ears.

"I'm still not used to the idea of being a daddy," George said.

"You'll get used to it, George," said Rider. "You'll do just fine, and you'll like it, too."

"Yeah. And if I ever need any pointers, I'll just come to you for advice."

"I just hope it don't look like you, George. I hope it looks like Lee."

They talked, small talk, until the sun began to turn purple. Then Rider called the children and sent them into the house. They protested a little, but they obeyed. Rider and George continued to chat, sometimes sitting for long silent moments, until the sun was well down. It was not a dark night, though, for the moon was bright and the stars were out. Finally Exie and Lee came out of the house.

"George," said Lee, "I think it's about time we were going home, don't you?"

George stood up and walked to her side. He took her by the arm.

"Yeah," he said. "You probably need to be getting to bed. You need your rest."

Lee looked at Exie, smiled and shrugged, as if to say, "You see? That's what I was telling you about." Then both women laughed a little.

"Good night," said Lee, "and thank you so much."

"Yes," said George. "Thanks. It was a great meal and a very pleasant evening."

"See you in the morning, George," said Rider.

George walked with Lee toward the buggy, which waited at the side of the road. He had insisted on renting the buggy so he could drive Lee to and from the Riders'. She had said that she was perfectly capable of walking, that she preferred walking even, but George had insisted on the buggy.

He helped her up into the seat and started around to the other side. He had just grasped the buggy with both hands and had one foot up. He was in the process of pulling himself up onto the seat when the gray pup barked loud and long and viciously. It startled George, and he looked past Lee toward the dog. Rider had just turned in reaction to the dog's bark. Beyond Rider, at the edge of the bluff behind the house, loomed a silhouette. It took a moment for the form to register on George's mind: a man holding to his shoulder a long gun.

"Rider," he called. "Look out!"

He had no time to go for his gun, and even if he could have gotten it out in time, the distance was too great. Lee was in front of him, and Rider was between him and the mysterious form. And Rider was unarmed. George recalled all of this in a flash.

Rider, too, saw the form, and he threw himself to the ground. A rifle cracked, but something was wrong. The sound came from somewhere behind George's back, and an instant later a shotgun blast roared. As the shotgun flashed in the night, the form at the edge of the bluff jerked, and its shot went up into the air. The body went back over the edge.

George looked over his shoulder, and he saw another mysterious figure emerge from shadow and walk out into Bluff Avenue. George squinted until the form came closer.

"Beehunter?" he said.

The three lawmen walked to the edge of the bluff and looked over. It was too dark to see. George helped Lee back down from the buggy, and she went back into the house with Exie. Rider got a lantern and lit it. He took the lantern, and he and George got into the buggy. Beehunter had his horse tied up on the other side of the street. They took the road south down the bluff and then back north until they were just beneath Rider's house. The gray pup followed along.

"Come on," said Rider. He took the lantern and led the way to the edge of Wolfe Creek. He held the lantern up high, but it still did not throw its light far enough. The pup barked and splashed into the creek. Rider waded in after it, crossing to the other side. George and Beehunter followed. At the base of the bluff on the other side of the creek, they found the body, twisted and broken, lying on its face. The shotgun lay a few feet away. Rider stepped up close holding the lantern, and Beehunter, with the toe of a boot, rolled the body over.

"Rider," said George. "Is it — ?"

"Yeah, George," said Rider. "It sure is. It's Matthew Thomson."

"Well, you told me we'd get him," said George.

Rider nodded.

"Yeah," he said. "Sooner or later. Why don't you go find some help to take care of this body. I'm going back up to the house and ask Exie for some good meat scraps to feed old pup here."